BURN SEASON

Also by John Lantigua

Heat Lightning

BURN

SEASON

John Lantigua

G. P. PUTNAM'S SONS
New York

Thanks to those friends in Costa Rica who helped in the research of
this book.

G. P. Putnam's Sons
Publishers Since 1838
200 Madison Avenue
New York, NY 10016

Designed by Sheree L. Goodman

Library of Congress Cataloging-in-Publication Data

Lantigua, John.
  Burn season / John Lantigua.
    p. cm.
  ISBN 0-399-13471-9
  I. Title.
PS3562.A57B87   1989   89-10135 CIP
813'.54—dc2

Printed in the United States of America

1 2 3 4 5 6 7 8 9 10

To Douglas, Edwina, and Ana Gioconda.

Chapter

—1—

I<small>T</small> was the night they killed off Topo. That was a Wednesday, a slow night. A few tables were full with my regulars and, in the corner, a group of Nicaraguan exiles. The Nicaraguans always sat in that corner by themselves, talking over what they had to talk over.

It hadn't rained that day and the air was thick with heat and humidity. The ceiling fans cut through it slowly as if they were under water. On the sound system, Celia Cruz was singing about the moon over Matanzas Bay, and out on the dance floor a half dozen couples drifted around, caught in the lazy currents of the song. In the back the French doors were open to the small casino, and a couple of old white-haired Chinamen sat hunched over the roulette wheel watching the black ball spin. They never got excited, the Chinamen, winning or losing. A nod or a grunt was all you ever got out of them. Each spin of the wheel was a small part of some complex system of luck they were spending a lifetime figuring out.

Me, I couldn't complain about my luck—I had a nice business there in Costa Rica. I did a good trade in local people all year round and I drew tourists during the season. I also attracted customers from around Central America, especially lately. As things got bad everyplace else, people showed up in Costa Rica. I got Honduran colonels masquerading as civilians, down for a bit of rest and relaxation. There were Salvadoran rebels who wore suits and carried briefcases, and who were in town for supposedly secret meetings. Panamanians came north trying to get away from the troubles in that country, and, of course, our neighbors the Nicaraguans who were on one side or the other of the Contra war.

There were exiled Cubans too, and South Americans, some of whom were CIA, or all of them, maybe. I didn't ask. I got arms dealers from Miami, emerald salesmen from Colombia, and journalists from here to Timbuktu. Everybody came to Costa Rica. It had palm trees, good fishing, and nice weather, even with the rainy season. It was also considered neutral ground, the only country around where people weren't shooting at each other. At least, until that night.

Lots of these same people came to "The Tropical Club," Jack Lacey, proprietor. I had a good location just off the main drags downtown in the capital city of San José and, for my money, the classiest place in town. I served clean food, and booze that wasn't watered down. At least not by me; I can't speak for the suppliers. The music was good and on the weekends we put on the best floor show this side of Mexico City or Havana. Like other clubs in San José, there was the casino, perfectly legal, and the wheel wasn't fixed or the dice loaded. Also, I minded my own business, although in a place like mine, you couldn't help but pick up a thing or two.

What I'd picked up during ten years in Central America, especially in the club, was that, despite all the trouble, everybody knew each other. There was bad blood between governments; armies or rebels crossing borders, shooting, sneaking back. There was always talk of breaking off relations and even countries going to war. It reminded me of New York where I grew up and the street gangs. From one block to the next people weren't that different, but still there were turf wars. And just like in New York, there were people in Central America who kept doing business with one another in the middle of the rumbles. Behind the scenes maybe, but they did. Family members, businessmen, colonels, politicians, diplomats, bishops, you name it. They had been in touch over the centuries and they still were. Making deals, making love, making hay. Sometimes they bumped into each other at my place, sometimes someplace else. But they did.

Just like I knew Topo, from way back, although I hadn't seen him in a while. He walked in, went right to the bar, and I watched him throw back a shot and ask for another. I was sitting across the way at my own table in the alcove next to the office, drinking *mojitos* with two friends of mine. One was Ray Reed, who was the assistant manager of the club. Ray's real name was Raimundo and he'd been born on the Caribbean side of Costa Rica. Ray was tall, black and broad-shouldered with a big Afro haircut. He had a quick smile, and when he flashed it, it looked like the beam from a lighthouse. His Caribbean accent made everything he said sound like Jamaican steel drum music. He had worked as a stevedore foreman on the docks over in Limón until he had an accident and lost a hand. He wore a metal prong on there now. Ray spoke both English and Spanish, was good with the customers, and the hook made him a bouncer people didn't mess with.

The other person drinking with us was a French journalist named Claude Renard. He was a tall, thin, high-strung guy, about forty, with black hair, sharp features and skin that, despite the tropical climate, was always dead white. That was because he spent almost all his time in places like mine, trading gossip. He had been in Central America about fifteen years and knew everything and everybody. He made regular trips all through the region and when he got back to Costa Rica he always stopped in. He soaked up whiskey and information in equal doses.

Right then he was drinking rum and watching a tall black girl in a tight skirt who was dancing by herself, her shoulders and hips in slow, perfect rhythm, her eyes closed.

"That is very nice," Renard said with his French accent and a mischievous lift of his eyebrows.

I glanced at the girl.

"I think that's Ray's cousin. He has a few dozen cousins in San José and they show up here."

Ray squinted at the girl as if he wasn't sure.

"Maybe she is one of them," he said.

Renard turned to him. "Excuse me, Raimundo. I didn't mean to show any disrespect for your family."

Ray smiled and shook him off.

"She's a big girl, mon. She order her own cock-tails."

Renard glanced at the girl again, sighed and shook his head.

"It's a shame I have work to do," he said. He turned

to me then. "So, Jacques, what's happening in San José that no one wants me to know?"

I sipped my drink. "The bougainvillea is flowering," I told him.

He tapped his finger on the table and his eyebrows flicked up like a typewriter carriage shifting to capitals.

"I'm sure that's not all that's flowering," he said lightly.

"I'm afraid that's my only hot tip."

He got a dreamy look on his face and stared into his cigarette smoke.

"You know, Jacques, I wish I were a nature writer instead of a political correspondent. Then I could write many beautiful things about the landscape of Mexico and Central America. About the bougainvillea." The look in his eyes was now bordering on the mystical. He stretched out a hand and sketched what he was seeing. "I could work for the *National Geographic* and write about the gorgeous Mexican sierra and the beautiful Guatemalan coffee highlands, the lakes and volcanoes in Nicaragua, the beaches of Costa Rica. That would be nice. For once, I could go into the countryside, searching for rare birds and flowers—instead of looking for the sites of battles and massacres."

"Maybe you can create a new career for yourself," I said. "You could specialize in tropical plants."

The faraway vision faded before his eyes and Renard got his usual skeptical squint. He sipped his rum, puckered his mouth and shook his head.

"Unfortunately it's impossible. I'm too much of a cynic, Jacques. The only animals who interest me are political animals. The only plants are the kind that the CIA plants."

He shrugged and tasted his drink again.

"Well, you could specialize in predators," I said.

Now he got a calculating expression, which wasn't unusual for him.

"The political landscape is very interesting these days," he said. "I have been in Mexico, Salvador, Honduras, Nicaragua lately. There are people who report that peace may be breaking out all over—as you gringos say. And just as the rainy season starts, as if the rain were making it grow. Isn't that something."

"There's your first nature story," I said.

"There are pressures being exerted for peace," he said. "There is much fatigue from the years of war, especially in Salvador and Nicaragua. And with your current administration coming to an end, they say there are certain meetings taking place, conversations, secret communications that cross borders. Of course, there are still accusations being made in public, but they serve only to cloud the truth."

He sipped his drink. He said all this in a tone that let you know he didn't believe it himself. There was as much chance of peace breaking out, as far as he was concerned, as there was of him writing about flowers.

"So you're betting on peace," Ray said, playing the straight man.

Renard shrugged.

"Of course, that's only what some people believe," he said with an ironic glance our way. "In other ways, nothing has changed. In Mexico, another election was just stolen. Of course in Mexico, if it wasn't stolen it wasn't an election."

"Of course," I said.

"In Salvador, what I found in the landscape were the bodies of young men with every bone broken.

14

They were pushed out of a helicopter, the people say. They saw them fall and heard the screams. I assume they were being interrogated, they were found guilty and sentenced on the spot. The army officers were identified, but nothing was done to them. So nothing has changed drastically there."

Ray took a taste of his drink as if to wash the story down.

"The Salvadorans they dancin' with death," he said. "They been doin' it for years."

"In Honduras, they've started to use human fertilizer as well," Renard continued. "I remember when the Hondurans used to be proud that they never killed each other over politics. In Nicaragua, no one has told the men holding the rifles that peace is breaking out. No one has told the refugees either. They still sneak from one country to another, that is if they can make it across the mountains and river borders without being shot. The Guatemalans go to Mexico, the Salvadorans to Guatemala and Honduras, the Nicaraguans come here. God knows why they bother to go from one place to another. And of course it will all get that much worse if there is any kind of escalation."

He went to his drink again and stared out at the dance floor where the couples were dancing a merengue.

"Always a bundle of joy, you are," I said.

He looked down his sharp nose at me.

"You ask, so I tell you, Jacques."

"So what's doing in Nicaragua?" I asked.

Renard looked at me and smiled his miserly smile.

"You are like me, Jacques. Nicaragua is your favorite. Maybe because of its beautiful women." His cynicism misted over again. "When I no longer go there, I will be nostalgic for it. It was my first assignment in

Central America, the Managua earthquake of nine-teen seventy-two. That's why maybe I am fond of it. And then of course I covered the insurrection and now the Contra war."

"The Nicaraguans, they are unlucky," Ray said. "Either the earth shake underneath them or someone drop bombs from the sky."

Renard sipped his drink, puckered and squinted into the distance. "Managua. They still haven't rebuilt it. There are buildings there in the center of town where there is jungle growing through the floor and up to the ceiling. You understand, the people on the out-side and the jungle on the inside. But you've seen all that, haven't you, Jacques?"

I nodded.

"Yes, I saw it years back."

Renard shook his head, drank and went on.

"What is going on there now is that in the northern mountains and in the southern part of the country towards Costa Rica they are still killing each other. It is a guerrilla war coming to an end. The Sandinistas feel if they can make it through these last months, maybe a new U.S. administration will not continue the policy. One leader up there told me, 'We are ready to let someone else be in the headlines of the American newspapers.' "

"That sounds smart of him," I said.

"The Soviets don't seem to want this war to con-tinue either," Renard said. "Third World adventur-ism appears on the decline. The great battle between East and West will end, at least in this corner of the world. Nicaragua will no longer be discussed at the summits, in fact it will be forgotten, which is possibly what they really want. And I'll have no excuse to keep on returning there and continuing my international relations with Nicaraguan women, who are some of the most beautiful in the world."

He shook his head, sighed and drank. Ray smiled. Renard looked at me.

"You have never been back, have you?" he asked.

"No."

"It's strange, Jacques, given your service during the insurrection."

I sipped my *mojito* and puckered from the lime.

"A lot of people in Costa Rica helped get rid of Somoza," I said. "People here don't like dictators."

He nodded.

"Yes, but not everyone actually picked up a rifle, became a guerrilla and went to fight against Somoza. Not everyone risked getting killed."

"Jack he was a brave boy," Ray said.

The conversation was getting uncomfortable. Renard and I had talked about this all before, but he had put away a few drinks and he was going over old ground. He should have known better. These days the Costa Ricans and Sandinistas didn't get along at all, and the last thing you needed in San José was to remind people that you had once fought in the Nicaraguan mountains.

"I told you before I had nothing better to do at the time," I said. "I was drifting through Costa Rica and they talked me into it. It was nothing more than that."

"And now?"

"Now I have better things to do. I work on my fishing and on keeping my tan in shape," I said. "I don't get mixed up in politics anymore. I run a business. And right now you'll have to excuse me because I have to tend the store."

Renard lifted his drink to me in a toast. Ray and I got up then and crossed the room. As I walked by the casino I saw another regular of mine sitting at the blackjack table, an American pilot named Chelly. He worked for a small cargo outfit out of Miami and people said he flew arms shipments for the CIA and delivered them to the Contras. According to Chelly, he'd flown helicopters in Vietnam and after the war ended he began flying anything, anywhere, for anybody who had the money. He once told me about flying freshly slaughtered meat over the Andes Mountains to the coast of Bolivia in bad rainstorms. The old, overloaded crate of a plane barely scraped over the mountain peaks and the meat piled right behind him was still warm and twitching.

Chelly twitched a bit himself. He was tall, skinny, pale, with a pair of extremely blue eyes. He had the wild blue yonder in him and probably some cocaine as well. He said hello as I went by and I gave him a wave.

Then I went over to the bar and talked to Paco, the head bartender. Friday and Saturday nights we had the floor show on, starring Isla Vega and her Caribbean Current, and we would pack them in. We needed enough booze back in the locker, enough steaks, lobster and shrimp. I had to make sure we had enough money in the safe to cover the casino, that the full contingent of waiters was scheduled and that they would all be sober. I had to make sure Ray had gotten the off-duty cops to guard the cars outside, to keep the hookers away from the entrance and to keep an eye on the band to make sure they weren't doing anything they shouldn't. I had to order a mountain of ice and keep it cold, which in the tropics was a trick.

I was still seeing to all that when Chico, the headwaiter, came over.

"Topo asked if you'll go to his table. He said he needs to talk to you."

I looked and saw Topo sitting by himself at a table at the opposite side of the room and I went over that way. Topo wasn't one of my favorite characters. He was a dark, nervous guy with a beaked nose and eyes that were always moving. I'd met him in 1979, just after the Sandinista victory. The way I understood it, he was half Costa Rican and half Nicaraguan and had family in both countries. During the last year of the Sandinista insurrection he had worked as an undercover agent for them on either side of that border, it being easy for him to travel both ways.

After the war ended, Topo had drifted around a bit, getting mixed up with anything and anybody where he could make a buck. Some people said he was still a Sandinista spy, others that he worked for the Costa Rican intelligence or even for the CIA. He'd sold some Colombian emeralds and did business in stolen passports. That's what people said. I wasn't very friendly with him when he came to the club so he didn't come much. He was a guy whose left hand didn't know what the right was doing. I didn't really want to know what either hand was doing, although I shook his right hand when he stood up and offered it.

"Hello, Jack. It's very good to see you," he said, but he had this nervous look in his eyes as if it weren't so good.

He pulled out a chair for me and I sat down.

"What can I do for you, Topo? I'm busy," I said, although I'm sure I didn't look busy at all.

Topo sipped his drink and his hand shook a bit.

"It's kind of you to give me an audience, Jack. But then we have been friends a long time," he said.

I shrugged. "We've known each other awhile."

He nodded enthusiastically. I glanced away. On the dance floor the black girl, Ray's cousin, was dancing to a reggae number, her body moving slowly and languidly like a palm tree bending in the wind.

"Since nineteen seventy-nine, that was the beginning," Topo said, and I turned back to him. "Those times were very exciting. We lived through important events, Jack. We worked together."

"We happened to be on the same side back then, yes," I said, with the accent on "happened."

He was still nodding at me with his sharp nose, his eyes darting around the room, to the corner where the Nicaraguans talked, then to the door and back to me.

"We knew some characters back then, Jack. Didn't we? And since then too." He leaned forward then and he fixed on my eyes, at least as much as his jittery little eyes could fix on anything. "If any of those characters were to come here looking for me you would tell me, wouldn't you, Jack?"

I frowned then. I wasn't sure what the story was, although it was pretty clear that Topo wasn't just nervous, he was scared. He had a split in his front teeth, and a nervous little ball of saliva quivered on his lip.

"Has anyone been here asking for me?" he asked.

"Not that I know," I said. He looked me in the eyes and nodded, but I could tell he didn't believe me. He kept nodding at me, searching behind my gaze for somebody hiding there. Then he drained his drink, motioned to Chico and ordered another.

He leaned forward and talked in a whisper.

"Big things are happening here, Jack, important things. There are some people around here," he said. His eyes went to the door as if those people were about to walk in and then he glanced back again. He looked at my eyes and I thought now he would cry. "I have an argument with some people, Jack. It's no good. I found some things out and they don't like it. They are looking for me, but I know you'll help me."

He nodded, as much for himself as for me, and got this twisted little smile on his face over the scared eyes. I shook my head.

"I don't get involved in politics, Topo. If you're in trouble with friends of yours, you'll have to straighten it out yourself."

He shook his head and looked dismayed.

"They are not friends of mine."

"Then I'd go to the police."

Topo looked more dismayed.

"I can't do that. Then for sure they kill me."

I frowned again. Topo was laying it on thick.

"All I need is a place to stay, Jack."

I shook my head.

"You can't stay here, Topo."

"Not here, maybe your house. That is out of town. No one will look for me there."

I was still shaking my head.

"If you need some money, I can lend you that. I don't need to know what you do with it. You buy a plane ticket if you want. I won't know where you went, so I won't be able to tell anybody."

"I don't need money, Jack."

I sipped my *mojito*.

"And I don't need trouble," I told him.

"I know I haven't always told the truth, Jack, and that I do some things you don't like, but I have never tried to fool you or lie to you. Still, you are willing to betray me now."

I lowered my drink then and just stayed looking at him. Topo had a crook's brand of honesty. He made it sound like being a bum was a decision of conscience on his part and you were the one without scruples for not helping him.

Right then the Nicaraguans in the corner all got up from their table and drifted across the dance floor, towards the door. Topo froze and watched them suspiciously until they were safely out. The drink went to his lips and some of it splashed on the table. He was desperate now, his voice quavering as he leaned towards me.

"Remember Hill One-sixteen, Jack," he said. "Hill One-sixteen."

The hills near the Costa Rican–Nicaraguan border, where Somoza's troops were finally beaten in 1979, were given numbers back then by the Sandinista military commanders. Maybe Topo had heard about a battle there, but I had been someplace else farther north. It was like Topo to have it wrong.

"I wasn't there, Topo. You have the wrong guy."

He stayed staring at me as if I was trying to fool him. His little hands were bunched in fists now. And then he played his last card. He leaned close to me, stared into my eyes and said:

"You should help me, Jack. Victor would want you to help me."

I looked at him and he lifted his eyebrows meaningfully. I looked into his eyes, one a lot smaller than the other and both of them full of lies.

"I haven't seen Victor Mena in nine years and I don't think you have either," I said.

"Victor was the contact for both of us during the war. We were all in it together. You know he would want you to help me. He does want you to help me."

I watched him a moment. You could smell the fear on his skin. Then I pushed the chair back and stood up.

"I told you I don't get mixed up in politics anymore, especially those kinds of politics, and I don't want anybody thinking I do or trying to get me involved. I don't want the trouble. Whatever plots you get mixed up in are your business, but don't come back in here anymore, they won't let you in."

Topo looked up at me. He looked hurt at first and then he got that twisted little smile. A sad, knowing smile.

"Don't worry, Jack. You don't have to concern yourself about that. I won't be back," he said. "You won't see me ever again."

Then he brought his drink up and gulped at it.

I went back to my table over in the corner and sat down next to Renard.

"Topo has had too much to drink?" he asked.

I glanced at him over the rim of my glass.

"I didn't know you were acquainted."

"Oh, yes. We met back in nineteen seventy-nine. He tried to sell me his account of being in the Sandinista underground. Since other people were telling me the same stories for free, I didn't buy it. Later, a few years ago, he tried to sell me some Colombian emeralds. Not very good emeralds. I didn't buy them."

I shrugged.

"He just tried to sell me something I didn't buy either," I said.

Renard pulled out his wallet, put a bill on the table and got up.

"Well, I'm going to buy my drinks and go home. I'm off to the northern border in the morning."

"Anything interesting?"

He flicked his eyebrows.

"You never know."

I walked him to the door.

"Have you heard from the daughter lately?" I asked him.

He looked at me and his eyes were bright now, not skeptical. Renard had a daughter in Italy from an "international affair" long ago. She was in her teens and lived with her mother. He had shown me a photo once, a girl in pigtails who looked like him, except healthier and she didn't have the cynical squint.

"We are meeting in Paris again in September." He said it as if it were a love affair he was carrying on. We were in July. "That's why I have myself on a deadline to get these latest stories out."

He waved goodbye and I watched him get in a cab and drive away. I went over and finished my *mojito* at the bar with Ray. After a while, I saw Topo get up and, zigzagging just a bit, make the door and go out. He didn't look back. It was just midnight. I sat back and watched that same long-legged black girl dance. Maybe Ray had it wrong, maybe she wasn't his cousin. She was facing me now, moving with that same lazy rhythm, her eyes smiling at me from under sleepy lids.

That was when the explosion came. It knocked the black girl clean off her feet, blew in the window at the front entrance, broke the mirror behind the bar and knocked my life out of whack but good.

Chapter

—2—

TWENTY minutes later
there was an army of cops in the parking lot, in the
street and in The Tropical. That's not exactly the kind
of clientele I wanted, but there was nothing I could
do about it.

Right after the bomb went off I ran outside with
Ray. We found the car on fire, flames shooting out of
the inside. The explosion had lifted it and moved it a
few feet. Underneath where it had been, there was a
hole in the pavement about the size a small mortar
would make. Topo was still behind the wheel, more
or less, what was left of him, what you could see
through the flames. Ray wanted to try to get him out,
maybe get his hook into his clothes and drag him free.
But I held him back. No sense trying to be a hero
when a guy was that dead.

I looked up the street. The blast had not only broken windows in my place and the mirror, it had

knocked letters off the marquee of the theater across the street and left an unintelligible garble of Spanish. It also blew out windows in the hotel next to that, and some of the guests were on the street now, men in undershirts, women in hair curlers. One of the prostitutes who hung out across the street had taken some glass, or maybe a small piece of the bomb, in her leg. She was on the ground and all the other whores were taking care of her, ripping off a piece of slip, tying a tourniquet like a bunch of Latin Florence Nightingales. I told them to bring her into The Tropical until the ambulance came. I had my policies against hookers, but there were times for exceptions. I stayed out there until a fire engine came and started dousing the flaming car.

I was back inside the club, assessing the damage, when Commissioner Eddie Pasos of the Costa Rican Ministry of Public Security came in. Costa Rica has no army and the ministry serves as a combination National Guard, FBI and CIA all rolled into one. The party in power put its own people in to run it and Eddie had been on the right side of the political battles over the past few years. His rank was equivalent to a major and that made him one of the top uniformed honchos in the country.

He was a short, compact, light-complected guy, with a carefully trimmed moustache. Natty, you'd call him. Eddie was also a bit chilly, smug, but no dummy. And he was honest as far as anybody knew. He came from a family of landholders of Spanish blood who were smart enough to back the civilian rebellion in the forties that had abolished the army. He was as Spanish as the black wrought-iron bars over the windows of the houses in San José, and just about as trusting.

We shook hands and he looked around.

"This is very unfortunate, Jack," he said. "Any idea who did it?"

"No, I don't."

Eddie watched me closely. Back in the early eighties, when the Costa Ricans and Sandinistas had stopped being buddies, Eddie had gotten very suspicious of me. There I was, a foreigner and a former foot soldier in the Sandinista insurrection, doing business in San José. So some of his plainclothes boys started hanging out at the club. Of course, they didn't turn up anything because I was clean. After a while Eddie left me alone, and even came to the club from time to time. He usually got a mischievous look on his face when he saw me and he said he came around to keep an eye on me.

I took him back to my office behind the dance floor, where I kept a small private bar.

"Are you on duty?" I asked.

"Yes, but I'll take a scotch on the rocks," he said. Eddie spoke precise English with only a twist of an accent.

He unbuttoned the bottom button of his uniform coat and sat on the couch. I brought him his drink and then sat myself behind the desk.

"I'm told Topo was in here drinking quite a bit before this . . . act of sabotage killed him," he said.

"That's right. With all respect for the dead, he was a bit bombed even before he went out the door," I said.

He squinted at me. "This isn't funny, Jack."

"You're telling me, *amigo*. I don't like explosions in my parking lot. It's bad for business."

Eddie sipped his whiskey and licked his thin aristocratic lips.

"I'm surprised you're not mourning for Topo, Jack. After all, he was a fellow combatant in the insurrection."

"So he was always telling me. All I know is he didn't fight in my unit in Nicaragua and now when he decides to get killed he does it outside my place when he could have picked somewhere else."

Eddie's gaze narrowed.

"I take it you didn't like Topo."

I shook my head.

"*Muy poco*," I said.

"Did you talk to him tonight?"

Eddie asked the question offhand as he crossed his legs, but I could tell he already had the answer. Maybe he was trying to ambush me.

"Yes, I did," I said. "He asked me to sit down with him. He wanted company."

"And what did he say to you?"

"He said he had some enemies and he was afraid they might try and kill him."

Eddie's slim moustache twitched with interest.

"Who were the enemies he was talking about?"

I shook him off.

"He didn't give me that piece of intelligence, but given all the different operations Topo was mixed up in, it might have been anybody. Even you, Eddie."

Eddie frowned. "That isn't humorous."

I shrugged. "They say Topo sold information to everybody, including Costa Rican intelligence. I'm just speculating."

Eddie sipped his whiskey. This was a little tit for tat. If he wanted to connect me to Topo for something that had gone on nine years before, I could connect him as well.

There was a knock on the door then. I got up,

28

opened it, and one of Eddie's lieutenants came in. He said the firemen had gotten the flames out and the police ambulance was there. Eddie told him he would supervise the removal of the body from the car, to wait for him. The other officer saluted and went out. Eddie went to the bar, poured himself another drink and sat down again.

"You weren't war comrades, but Topo still came to see you?"

"He wanted me to hide him out, to give him some cover from his enemies."

"And what was your response?"

I shook my head. "I told him no. I told him I don't get mixed up in politics."

Interest sparked again in Eddie's eyes.

"You think Topo was eliminated for political reasons. He was also mixed up with common criminals. Why not them?"

I shrugged.

"Topo was a guy who had a talent for making enemies. Too much playing everybody against the middle. Who knows who did it?"

Eddie thought that over.

"Did he tell you where he was going when he left here?"

"No. I told him maybe he should blow the country. But he didn't want to do that."

Eddie nodded, but behind his eyes, wheels were turning.

"He told you he was afraid he would be killed?"

"That's right."

"And you still told him you couldn't help him. That wasn't very Christian of you, Jack."

I didn't like the tone of voice. It was as if maybe I had something to do with Topo getting hit.

"I didn't believe him," I said. "Topo wasn't always believable. And like I told you, I didn't like him."

Eddie drank that in.

"And that was all he said to you?"

I hesitated for just a moment and Eddie looked at me like a sniper taking a bead on someone.

"That's all," I said. I wasn't about to tell him that Topo had mentioned a Sandinista state security officer. I didn't need to have my name connected to Topo to begin with, but much less the enemy to the north, especially when I hadn't had any contact with Victor Mena in nine years. And especially when I didn't believe Topo in the first place.

Eddie kept his eyes trained on me, as if somehow he knew what I was holding back. He must have figured I knew more than I was saying, but that I didn't need to make enemies and have somebody coming after me. That I didn't want to get caught in the middle, because in Central America the middle was a very dangerous place to be.

Eddie sipped his drink and ran a finger over his thin moustache. It was probably 2 A.M. and he looked fatigued. His accent got heavier when he was tired. He was gazing down into his whiskey.

"You know, Jack, we don't like battles on our streets here in San José. We don't want our country becoming a theater of war, other people's war. We guard our neutrality."

"I know. That's why I do business here. I don't like tending bar in a combat zone either. I used to do it in New York."

Eddie nodded, but didn't smile.

"We are a very small country, Jack," he said. "There are less than three millions of us. Just your city of New York has many more people than we do." He sipped his drink and looked at the wall in front of him as if he could see through it. "We want to be open to foreigners, and we want to offer them and our citizens a free society, a life in peace, all the guarantees."

I didn't say anything. Then he met my eyes and his gaze sharpened considerably.

"But given the current situation in the region, we must think first of survival, Jack. I believe you understand that," he said. "A person of your background, your history, Jack, has to be especially careful. There are old allegiances, old friendships that one can't forget. But you should remember that now you are part of this country, you do business in Costa Rica, and you would not want to be involved in anything that is not in our interest. You would not want to cause us trouble."

This wasn't Eddie the gentleman now, this was Eddie the cop. His eyes were as narrow as bayonets and his words had taken on a very cool edge.

I nodded.

"I'm past thirty-five," I told him. "I can't be drafted and I'm not about to enlist in any war, especially somebody else's, not anymore."

He nodded patiently.

"That is very good, Jack," he said. "Just remember what I told you. Keep in mind your interests and ours."

He drained his drink then and got up.

"And if you remember anything else Topo said to you please report to me."

He gave me that same mischievous look he always gave me, except now I didn't like it. We shook hands and went out.

The cops had cleared out of the bar so that it no longer looked like a barracks. I did some cleaning up.

When I got outside, the body had been taken away, but the car was still there. It was a mess. It was twisted and charred and the four tires were just black puddles of rubber on the pavement.

Then the news photographers and cameramen arrived, a small battalion of them. A couple of reporters came up, but I told them I knew nothing and they should ask the authorities. Eddie talked to them for a minute, got in his jeep and sped off, leaving a couple of his men on duty guarding the wreck.

I went back inside. Chico and the boys had cleaned up and gotten the place in order. They'd put some wood over the two shattered windows. I stood looking at the work and Ray came up.

"This isn't good, boss," he said to me. "That Topo, he was a bad bet."

"You're telling me."

"You have to be careful with this, play your cards right," he said now. "You don't know what's going on."

Ray's face was full of suspicion, as if he was up against a crooked roulette wheel. He was looking out for me, for us.

"Don't worry, we have nothing to do with it," I said. "Go home and get some rest."

I got ready myself to go. My night watchman, an old uncle of Ray's, looked a bit skittish, as if I were leaving him to guard headquarters by himself. I told him the two cops would be there with him and he calmed down. It was about 4 A.M. by the time I got in my own Land Cruiser and drove off. The smell of molten metal and burnt rubber was still in the air. That, and the heat.

Chapter

— 3 —

As it turned out, Eddie Pasos was just the first visitor I got over the next twenty-four hours who wanted to know all about the dead man, Topo Morales, and what he told me. Topo, it turned out, had quite a following.

I got about three hours' sleep and by the time I woke up the story was all over the radio. I listened to Eddie give the reporters the account I'd told him: what time Topo had come in, that he had gotten drunk, that he had told "the manager of The Tropical that he was afraid for his life" and then the bomb. I made a face at the radio when I heard that. I didn't need Eddie putting me at center stage in this tragedy. People in the entertainment business shouldn't get involved in tragedies, especially violent ones, it's bad for business.

Eddie also said that the body had been positively

identified through dental charts and fingerprints on
one unburnt hand and that the investigation was continuing.

I got up and found Jacoba, my old housekeeper,
standing in the kitchen, her hands clutching her
apron, staring at the radio as if it was about to blow
up. Then she looked at me as if I were a walking dead
man and blessed herself. Jacoba doesn't like bombs
going off anywhere nearby, especially near me.

"What is this that happened?" she asked me in
Spanish. There was an edge on her voice as if it was
my fault. I was the one who had set off the bomb.

"I don't have anything to do with it," I told her.

She threw her hands in the air then. "The world,
it's going crazy," she said and she started to mutter
about war and how it was everywhere, a plague that
would kill everyone.

I calmed her down after a while and got her to
make me eggs and some coffee. Then I showered and
shaved and drove down to the club.

I found a bunch of people standing around the
parking lot. The car was still there and they were staring at the hole the bomb had made, a small facsimile
of the Grand Canyon. They were tourists visiting the
latest attraction in San José. I went in and found Ray
and some workmen—more relatives of his—already
patching up the windows and fixing the lights above
the stage that had been blown out.

I got on the phone to Eddie Pasos's office, and was
told he was busy being interviewed by a Costa Rican
television crew, which was all I needed. I left a message that he should please get his "evidence," the car,
out of my lot and try to not put my name in the same
sentence with Topo or any other dead man.

That afternoon some of my regulars stopped by just

to make sure that the place was still standing and I stood them drinks at the bar so that they'd go back and tell people I was still in business. At midafternoon, two of the old Chinamen came in and went to the casino. That was reassuring. By happy hour the windows were replaced, I had the club open and, at least by the looks of it, back to normal.

At one o'clock, I went to relieve Pedro, my croupier at the roulette table. His regular relief hadn't shown up. I guess with the bomb going off he figured my luck had run out. I was still there when Ray came up with another guy, an older man who looked American.

"This gentleman he wants to see you," Ray said. He handed me a card; it said W. Richard Akers, Consular Section, United States Embassy. I handed Ray the roulette rake and shook Akers's hand.

He was a strange-looking man, small, probably sixty years old or older, with pure white hair, the whitest hair I'd ever seen. He wore it combed straight back off his forehead, sweeping behind his ears and falling down his neck in the back. Under that mane of hair, his face was small and pale, although it was chafed in spots as if he suffered from some skin condition. He had very small dark eyes, close together, on either side of a large hooked nose, and they blinked a lot. His mouth was small and he had no chin, so that his face just seemed to melt into his neck. He had on a black shirt, dark slacks and snappy white shoes that matched the color of his hair. When he spoke, his voice was sharp and nasal.

"I've just dropped in for a moment, Mr. Lacey," he said. "It's a pleasure to see you in one piece. We heard about the incident last night and the ambassador sent me right over to see if there was anything we can do to help."

"You thank the ambassador," I told him, "but we're back in business already."

"So I see," he said. His white head was swiveling slowly, stiffly, now from one side to the other as he scanned the room, his small round eyes blinking regularly, as if even the little light there was in the place bothered them. On either side of his nose there were indentations left by glasses. The marks looked like breathing holes in a bird's face. His gaze stopped at the crap table where there were a few players. He looked them over carefully and finally he came back to me.

"The ambassador was very concerned," he said. "In high-risk areas such as Central America, American businessmen can become prey for subversives. They can become free game for terrorists. He doesn't want to see that happen here."

"That makes two of us," I said.

"Amen," Ray said without lifting his eyes from the wheel.

One of the other croupiers brought me a draft to sign and I did. Akers stayed blinking at the roulette wheel where the ball spun, rattled and then finally hopped into a hole.

"Do you like to gamble, Mr. Akers?" I asked him.

He shook his head stiffly.

"Not often," he said, "but I take it you are a gambling man, Mr. Lacey. If you weren't, you wouldn't be in business in Central America."

I shrugged.

"All business is a gamble, no matter where you do it."

"But some more than others and some places have longer odds."

"I'll take my chances with Costa Rica," I said.

I expected him to give me the line I got from lots of people; that I was crazy to risk my money anywhere in Central America, that it was a bad bet these days with all the fighting. But he didn't. Of course, he was an American diplomat and Costa Rica was an ally. He nodded with quick nervous jerks.

"I'm with you, Mr. Lacey," he said. "The stakes we're playing for here are high. There is a battle going on between two systems of life in Central America. The other guys have tricks going on under the table. Subversion, car bombs. But I still think we'll take the pot."

He looked up at me and smiled cleverly now. It was a strange, awkward smile. It curved up on either side of his beaked nose.

"That's fine," I said.

"But you have to play cautiously, Mr. Lacey," he said, blinking at me. "Subversion is a very unpredictable activity. You never know where it's going to spread or who it will affect. In this case, you might attract unwanted attention. Someone might make certain wrong assumptions about you because of this bomb going off."

He put a little spin on the word "assumptions" that caught my interest. It caught Ray's interest too. He glanced at Akers and then back at the spinning ball.

"For instance," I said.

Akers thought and blinked across the dark casino.

"Someone might think this man, Morales, talked to you just before he died because you were mixed up with him in some business or other."

"I wasn't."

"Or they might believe that since you were the last person to talk to him, apparently, that he might have told you something important about those who had

37

reason to kill him. Information that might compromise you, be dangerous to you."

Ray grunted, but kept his eyes on the wheel.

"He didn't tell me a thing," I said. "It was just like I told the police. Nobody has any reason to be interested in me."

Akers stared at me now. When his eyes were steady he didn't look nervous or old. In fact, when he stopped blinking, his look was hard, even a bit cruel.

The ball clattered into a cup. Ray called it and raked in chips.

Akers was fixed on me.

"It's good to see a man with backbone, Mr. Lacey," he said. "Another man might get scared, want to sell out. Most people would want to cut and run."

"I'm staying," I said.

After a few moments, he nodded.

"That's good, Mr. Lacey. The ambassador will be very happy to hear that." He blinked at me a few more times and said, "Now I have to be going." He offered me his hand and I took it. "If you have any reason to call us, don't hesitate. We want you to know that we are concerned for your safety."

I said thank you to him again and then I saw him to the door of the club. He stood on the outside steps and blinked into the light.

He turned to me and said, "Don't bet any long shots, Mr. Lacey," and he gave me his strange smile again. Then the little man walked to a black car with diplomatic plates, got in and drove off.

Later on I remembered it was Akers who first suggested that I might sell The Tropical and fly the coop. That was before things got heavy and it became more than a suggestion.

* * *

38

I went back to the bar then. Over the next few hours I had to tell people the story about the bomb going off at least a half dozen times and then I had to feed the same people drinks so they'd forget about it. After a while I decided I'd take a break and go get a cup of coffee.

I went out into the light and walked a few blocks towards the center of town. Downtown San José looks like a city in a time warp; half the buildings are left over from the last century, one or two stories, with peeling paint and the red corrugated-tin roofs you see in the tropics, and the other half are new glassy office towers. It was about 5 P.M., the narrow sidewalks were full of working people heading home and the streets choked with cars and the humidity that came before a night when it was going to rain. I got to the central plaza with its big old whitewashed cathedral and tall palm trees and ducked in across the street to the Cafe Mundo.

It was a place with blue tiled arches that opened right on the sidewalk. You sat at an old scarred wooden table and watched the flow of humanity pass a couple of feet away. Working the archways themselves were the lottery sellers and the whispering men who offered foreigners the best black market rate for their dollars. Inside, the place smelled of coffee and faintly of grease. The walls were covered with glass cases full of sticky sugared pastries that looked like they might have been there an age. Overhead the ceiling fans moved fast enough to keep the flies on their toes.

I ordered coffee. The clientele was all men, huddled at tables talking. Shoeshine boys worked the crowd, kneeling underneath the tables and snapping their rags, and sometimes a guy drifted in with a guitar and

39

sang in Spanish. But now I was reading an afternoon paper I found on the table.

On the front page there was a color photo of the burnt car Topo had died in sitting in my parking lot. Just the kind of advertising I needed. The headline screamed, *"Club Nocturno Escena de Muerte Misteriosa,"* "Nightclub Scene of Mysterious Death." Wonderful. The club was mentioned another half dozen times in the story inside.

I was still sitting there reading, when suddenly there was a hand on my shoulder, a heavy hand. I looked up and there stood Pepe Esparza, another guy who it turned out had a special interest in Topo. He was a big, fat guy, bald on top and burnt red from the sun. He had this twenty-four-hour smile you figured he wore even in his sleep, and lots of gold in his teeth.

They called Pepe "the Dessert Man." He had once been a big cheese with the U.S. banana companies in Nicaragua and he had also owned interests in coffee and sugar. So they called him "the Dessert Man" not only because he ate a lot of it, but because that's what he exported to the United States. Bananas, coffee, sugar.

Then the Sandinistas won power and took over the banana plantations and Pepe's other holdings. So he sailed off to Miami where he got into real estate. He cut himself a sweet deal selling condos to the people from Nicaragua who were washing up in Florida. A couple of years back he had blown into San José as the press agent for the Contra boys. I guess he got tired of being in Miami waiting for somebody else to win back his bananas. Pepe put out press releases describing battles, Contra victories in the midst of the Nicaraguan jungles. Most of it he made up out of whole cloth, including the enemy body counts. But then the Sandinistas did the same thing. It was all part of modern warfare, winning the war in the newspapers.

It was rumored that Pepe also played a role in buying arms for the Contras and that he raked off a small commission. He liked to come to my club to sit down with the journalists and tourists and tell them that he would be playing golf in Managua again any day. He was a piece of work, Pepe. You could take the boy off the plantation but you couldn't take the banana out of the boy. He was still slippery.

Right now he was dressed in a large pink shirt with an alligator on it and white golf slacks. He had sweated in the shirt so it looked like the alligator might swim away. He was holding a banana daiquiri, which is all he ever drank.

"I'm glad to see you are all right, Jack," he said, squeezing my shoulder. "I hear you had some bad beezness at your place last night."

"That's exactly what it is, bad business," I told him.

Pepe nodded, the rolls of fat in his neck working like springs. He sat down then, the old wooden chair creaking dangerously under his weight. A waiter was going by; Pepe stopped him, and ordered a *prusiana*, a pastry filled with custard. Then he turned to me. Pepe had taken some business classes at one time in the U.S., and spoke English like a stock market tip sheet, but with a heavy accent.

"For my monies that is the bottom line, Jack," he said. "It is bad for beezness. We see this too in Miami. People they kill each other all the time. There it is the drug people. Three, four of them every week, they get their cheeps cashed in. It is not good for the beezness in Miami."

"You're not kidding," I said.

41

Pepe shook his head. It made his fat move and the change jingle in his pocket. He gulped down part of his banana daiquiri. Then he said to me, "This man Morales who was killed, they say he was a cheap cruke."

I was watching the Costa Rican working girls hurrying past, but Pepe saying that made me smile.

"I don't know," I said to him. "You would have to ask the men in your organization who did business with Topo. I can't say what he charged for his information, how cheap a 'cruke' he was."

Pepe's expression went sour.

"We don't associate with people like this, Jack."

"Then you were the only people around San José who didn't," I said. "Topo was mixed up with everybody. As a matter of fact, I've seen him in my club talking to some of your boys."

Pepe frowned and said nothing. Then the waiter came with his pastry. He bit into it, custard squirting out the side. By the time he had chewed and swallowed, he had decided to change tactics, to sweet-talk me. He dabbed at his lips with a napkin.

"Maybe we talk to him a leetle, Jack. He knows some people, but it is nothing important."

"You mean you did business with him, but not enough so that you had reason to kill him. That's what you're trying to sell me."

Pepe shook his head until he stopped chewing.

"I don't sell you nothing, Jack," he said. "But for us it is like for you, it is bad beezness that this happen in San José. People they start keeling and the Costa Ricans they throw us out of here. The stakes they are too high for that. That is the greety neety."

He meant the nitty gritty.

"So who do you think killed him?" I said.

42

Pepe held both hands out like fat scales of justice.

"There are many options," he said. "He was associated with many enterprises."

The way he said "enterprises" gave Topo's activities a distinctly illegal flavor. He leaned towards me. His breath smelled sweet.

"Maybe they kill him, his friends who sell emeralds," he said, "or maybe because of the phony passports or the whores for whom he is agent."

He chewed and watched me.

"Is that what you think?" I asked him.

He worked his tongue back along his teeth to dig out a piece of pastry and then he shook his head.

"No," he said, and he fixed on me. "I think he is killed by the Sandinistas."

I let surprise register on my face.

"No kidding."

Pepe's head bobbed as he chewed.

"I bet the rancho on it, Jack."

Of course, Pepe didn't have a rancho anymore, the Sandinistas had confiscated it. I sipped my coffee.

"And why would they do that? Why have Topo killed after all these years?"

Pepe dabbed at his lips.

"Because before Topo works for them, but now lately he talks to us. So they keel him."

I frowned.

"Why would they worry that he talked to you? He probably didn't know anything very valuable to sell you."

Pepe rolled his eyes and then looked at me out the side of them.

"Probably he doesn't, but maybe he does. Maybe something very interesting."

"Like what?"

He frowned, as if he'd gotten a curdle in his custard. I was being indiscreet. He said:

"Maybe Topo knows something and he tells us and not them. Everybody know the Sandinistas they are broke. They can do nothing for him."

He smiled cleverly at me. I studied that smile, the gold laid between teeth which were the yellow color of custard. Too much dessert. But what he said about Topo was true enough; he was the kind of guy who would sell out to the highest bidder. Although if he could do that and still make a small commission from the other side, he would do that too.

One of the shoeshine boys across the room snapped his rag so that it popped like a gunshot and Pepe looked up nervously. He frowned, then turned to me.

"It was them who keel him, Jack."

"Says you," I told him. "For all I know it might have been some of your boys trying out one of their bombs you buy for them. In fact, some of your boys were in my place last night and they left just before Topo went out to his car. I forgot to tell the cops that." I was just remembering it and it made me consider the Dessert Man more closely.

He chewed the last mouthful of pastry and washed it down with banana daiquiri. He worked his tongue over his teeth again and looked at me.

"Up in Miami there are boys who tell us they keel anybody we want," he said. "They will do it for a price. Very bad Cuban boys."

He stayed staring at me, not moving except for the bellows movement of his breathing. I sipped my coffee.

He screwed his head back and forth.

"But we don't run that kind of operation, Jack," he said. "We don't put the contracts on the people."

44

He nodded at me sincerely. "It is the trooth."

"I'm relieved to hear it, Pepe," I said.

He wet his finger and began to dab the last crumbs from the plate.

"In the insurrection you fought with the Sandinistas, Jack. Maybe you make a mistake back then, a bad investment. But now I think you are a smart beeznessman. You know who are your friends. You know who to do beezness with."

I watched him and the ceiling fan sawing overhead.

"People do business in different ways, Pepe."

He looked up at me and frowned, the fat on his forehead furrowing.

"Beezness is beezness, Jack." He said it as if he was stating one of the elemental laws of the earth, like gravity. "Maybe Topo he tell you something about what he is involved in. Maybe something that we should know."

Now we were getting down, as Pepe himself would say, to the greety neety. So maybe Topo really did have something to tell Pepe and his boys, but maybe he had gotten killed first. Pepe figured I knew what it was. I was thinking now about what Akers had tried to peddle me; about people thinking I knew more than I did.

I said:

"It's all on the radio, Pepe. Just like I told the cops. I'm a good citizen. I always tell the police everything."

Pepe licked the crumbs off his finger and sat and breathed at me a good ten seconds.

"Me too, Jack. I am a good citizen," he said finally. "And all my associates they are good citizens and good customers to you."

He tipped back his daiquiri then and drained it,

watching me over the frothy edge of the glass. He put it down, licked his lips, took out a bill that easily covered both our orders and hauled his bulk out of the chair. He smiled down at me.

"I have many contacts," he said. "When this is all over and we are back in Managua, we will open a Tropical Club there. Maybe we open one in Miami too."

I didn't say anything. The Dessert Man squeezed my shoulder.

"I am glad you aren't hurt, Jack," he said. "You are too sweet a man to be hurt." He patted my cheek, gave me his golden smile, and I watched him waddle out.

I got up myself then, went back to the club, put Ray in charge for the night and went home to get some sleep.

Chapter

—4—

PEOPLE always asked me how a guy from New York ended up doing business in Costa Rica in the first place. To explain that, I had to mention Nicaragua and the fact that I fought in the insurrection. When I told them that, they asked me how from one day to the next I could get myself mixed up in a guerrilla war. Not in my own country, on my own turf, but in a place I didn't even know. Get mixed up in somebody else's war.

Well, it was easy. I had a marriage that broke up in New York City one winter, broke up for good. I was working as assistant manager of a club in New York, over on the west side. It wasn't my place and the money wasn't that good. So I decided for a while I'd take off to some place that didn't seem quite as cold, in more ways than one. I decided on an extended vacation in Costa Rica, fishing, drinking and other things. What you might expect a guy recently split up to do.

Once I was there, I bumped into this guy from Nicaragua. His name was Carlos. We met at a cheap hotel where we were both staying and we got to know each other. Carlos liked to talk baseball and politics. In baseball, he was a Mets fan, and politically, he called himself a revolutionary. That's the word he used.

He told me how things were in his own country, Nicaragua, and how they had to change. I listened to him and I agreed with him. In San José those days you were always hearing about the Nicaraguan strongman, Somoza, and what a corrupt bastard he was. The changes Carlos talked about sounded right, giving everybody a fair shot.

He asked me about what I'd done before and what I had planned. I told him I'd come from not the best neighborhood in New York, had studied some and bounced around in a lot of things, but mostly the bar and restaurant business. I was twenty-seven years old, had just gotten divorced up there, and I was in Costa Rica on my own. I said I was looking for something new to do, maybe even a new life altogether.

So one night, after we've known each other a couple of weeks, he takes me to this bar and we got into a conversation with some friends of his. Except it wasn't barroom conversation like normal. It wasn't point spreads on basketball games and where to get a hot color TV. Carlos introduces me to these Nicaraguan friends of his who tell me about this other kind of scam they're up to. They're talking about going to war and freeing their country from this goon of a dictator, Somoza. They are perfectly serious about this.

When they talk about it they look a bit like the guys back home who have scams going. They want to convince you—and themselves—they can pull it off. In this case, all they need is a few more bodies to carry a few more guns.

Back home I've never gotten involved in the scams I hear in bars, but this scheme is different. It isn't to line my pockets, it's not to end up on Easy Street. They say it is to get rid of this fat cat of a dictator, to help the average guy in Nicaragua get back what belongs to him. They ask me what I know about Somoza and I tell what I've learned. I wouldn't call myself a revolutionary, but I tell them I think they're right to go after him. They say Somoza is on his way down at last, they're coming to the crunch. Any able man willing to fight they can use. A few other Americans had joined up and they ask me if I want to go in with them.

All the time we're talking I've been drinking, I'm pretty lit, and I'm ready to go right then. But they tell me to sleep it off, think about it and decide in the next day or two.

To tell the truth, at the moment, with the divorce and all, I'm up for anything, and I'm willing to take risks. If you want, I'm the perfect customer for them. On top of that, once you've even considered doing something like this, normal life seems just a bit dull. Anyway, I walk around San José for a day thinking and by sunset I'm decided I'm going.

That's what happened. That night I met Victor Mena and some of his buddies. Mena, he was the main man. He was older than the others, over forty, and more together. When he spoke, you didn't feel he was selling you something. You felt he was giving you a history lesson, like in school. The history of Nicaragua, of all Latin America. I don't remember it all now, but I remember Mena.

That first night they had asked me my full name and my old address up in the Bronx and a few other things. It turned out there were other exiled Nicaraguans up in New York who did some quick checking. They found out I wasn't some sort of infiltrating agent, trying to take them for a ride.

For a few days I did nothing but run errands. Then one day they moved me and Carlos out of the cheap hotel we were in and we went to start our training. Not in some army base, but in a safe house, still in San José, but outside the center of the city. The house looked like any respectable middle-class house in the suburbs, but the people who lived there were the Sandinista training officers. Some neighbors to have. They showed us, and four other guys I'd never seen before, how to take apart and put back together again an automatic rifle. I'd never seen one of those guns before, but then I understood why they were illegal. They shoot thirty rounds in about three seconds. They showed us how to hold it, move with it, shoot it, although there was no live ammunition so that the rifles were silent, like the shooting in a dream. They didn't want to rile up the neighbors. They showed us how to crawl on our stomachs without making noise, and also how to fight in close with a knife. It was like taking a lesson in mugging.

A week later—no more than that—we left behind the skyline of San José, and we were smuggled into Nicaragua. Carlos and I crossed the border in a car with a middle-class housewife from Managua who was a Sandinista collaborator. Carlos was a Nicaraguan citizen and showed his papers and I was an American tourist, as innocent as can be. The other guys were also smuggled in and we all met up at a safe house in Managua.

We spent only one night there. The next day, at dusk, the six of us and a driver squeezed into a car and headed up the highway towards the northern sierra. We drove almost three hours into the dark, then turned off onto a dirt road, went another half hour and then suddenly stopped. It was ten o'clock at night, no moon, dark as a cave, not a house in sight.

The driver turned off the headlights, waited a few moments, turned them on and off again three times. From a hillside just above the road, the blinks were answered.

"Everybody out," he said. We unloaded provisions we had brought in the trunk.

A minute later the driver and the car were gone, as if they had never been there. We were with a lone Sandinista guerrilla who had been sent to fetch us and take us to a camp deep in the mountains.

That day my life changed. That happens to just about anyone who becomes a soldier, you go from peace to war in a moment. For me it came out of the blue. Like turning a corner onto the wrong block.

Our guide was a guerrilla named Rigo, a very dark-skinned guy who had been in the mountains already a couple of years. He told us we would have to walk between a week and ten days to reach our unit, not exactly a stroll through Central Park.

He got us outfitted with equipment that had been dropped off in the same spot days before. We were each given a backpack with food, a plastic hammock, a rain poncho, extra provisions for the camp, an automatic rifle and ammunition. All told, we each carried about seventy-five pounds. It was what Rigo called "the cross," the cross each one had to carry to be a guerrilla.

We started to move that same night. Sometimes we walked only at night and slept during the day. At first you were like a baby, just learning. You were stumbling even crawling up hillsides. You talked too loud and Rigo had to tell you to be quiet. We walked up and down, again and again, much of the time not knowing what direction we were moving in. Sometimes there were stars overhead and sometimes the trees covered them and you couldn't see a thing. The hills became like waves and you felt you were at sea facing one wave after another. Blisters opened on my feet like I used to get playing basketball and my legs went from aching to just being numb, and then back again.

The first few days I hardly slept. I started seeing things. The bushes became people and turned back to bushes again. Adrenaline altered your perception. Fear, that is. Your nerves had to get in shape just like the rest of you. In New York, you had plenty to worry about at night, but not snakes or wildcats. For a city boy, this was like walking on another planet—or walking through a nightmare.

During your week in San José, they fed you very well. Not New York home cooking, but not bad. Still, they let you know once you were inside you would sometimes have an empty belly. And you better not complain about it. Once we were in the mountains we ate some dry tortillas we'd brought with us and dried meat. After that we foraged. We dug up yucca, we picked bananas and other fruit growing wild. Eight days into Nicaragua, Rigo shot a monkey. There were a bunch of them jumping around in the treetops above us. We knew we were far from civilization and there was no chance of the shot being heard by the enemy. He shot a good-sized monkey and it fell from its tree limb and landed just off the path. Even with the fall, it wasn't quite dead. It looked up at us with these too-human eyes. It was then that I knew what kind of a new world I was in. A long way from New York. There would be human beings at the other end of my rifle, people who would have the same look in their eyes, just before they died.

It took us the full ten days to get to the section of the sierra where we were assigned. During that time we had contact with a couple families, collaborators, but in general we avoided contact with the local residents. We sometimes saw houses on hillsides, or lights from lanterns at night, but we didn't go near them. There were six of us, besides Rigo: three Nicaraguans, including Carlos, two Costa Ricans and me. The guys you were with you knew only by their special war names, noms de guerre. Mine was Antonio. If any one of us was captured he couldn't divulge the real identities of the others. If the National Guard had those real names they would go harass or even kill family members of the Nicaraguans.

My Spanish got a lot better during that trip because we talked some, although when we weren't sleeping we were generally on the move. Where I grew up in the Bronx there were Spanish neighborhoods nearby and I knew some words from there, but not much. Now the Latin guys asked me about New York, the Statue of Liberty, the baseball teams and the women, mostly. Just the trip into Nicaragua was enough to create a bond between us. At one point, one of the new recruits, Felipe, got diarrhea, probably from drinking bad water. Then he developed a fever. He got delirious one afternoon. We had to carry him in a plastic hammock swung from poles. He chattered like a parrot while he was delirious. We took turns carrying him for two days until he got better. We stuck together that way.

It was on the eleventh day that we made contact with the unit we were meeting and that was where I met her.

It was a group of about two dozen camped on a hilltop. They told us the nearest town was about three hours' walk through the wilderness. They had been based there about a week and everyone had a spot he had hung his plastic hammock. It was like a miniature village. They had a central eating area. No cooking was done during the day because the smoke could attract the enemy. There were jobs to be done: finding food, keeping guard, mounting patrols, scouting and planning the next attacks.

The man in charge was called Candido and had been in the mountains six years. He was like the mayor of that makeshift town. Amongst the two dozen guerrillas there were three women. I met her at dinner that first night. She had been in a scouting party and had arrived back just before nightfall. The name they had given her was Lavinia.

She was in her early twenties and said she had been in the mountains just over a year. She was medium height, dark, pretty, quiet and serious. She wore an M-2 automatic rifle over her shoulder the way most women carry a purse. There were guys I grew up with who wouldn't have anything to do with Latin girls back then. Me, I didn't know any either, but it wasn't because I didn't find them attractive. That first night we ate beans and rice, that was it. We sat around the fire and she gave the report for the scouting party.

They said there was a company of National Guard bivouacked at a coffee plantation about ten kilometers away. They had been running patrols in that sector to protect certain plantations owned by friends of Somoza. They had also been harassing the local population, including some of our friends. In one case, a collaborator of ours had disappeared and was later found dead on the side of a road. Candido listened and said we couldn't let the *guardia* get away with that. We had to protect our people or they would lose faith. He decided we would try and ambush them if possible the next day. Three of the new guys, including Carlos and I, were assigned to the ambush party, a baptism of fire and initiation into the gang.

She and I ended up sitting next to each other at the fire. At one point our eyes met. She looked frankly into mine. It wasn't like the city where you looked at a girl and she looked away. She told me later that she had never taken a man since she'd come into the mountains.

The next day she was assigned to the same ten-man unit that was going to ambush the *guardia*. We moved about two hours before dawn, when it was still damned cold in those tropical mountains, and by the time the sunlight was visible behind the ridge to the east, we had reached our spot. We dug out spaces for ourselves in the vegetation about forty feet above a trail near the plantation, where we expected them to pass. It was a spot just after a curve in the trail where it would be almost impossible for them to see us, but would give us a clear shot at them. Once we were dug in, we kept dead quiet. We were about ten feet apart from each other. Carlos was on one side of me and she was on the other. You couldn't see the next person because of the thick foliage, but you sensed him or her there. The only sound was the birds and the monkeys in the trees.

In San José, I'd been instructed about ambushes. Victor Mena had said: "Guerrilla war is one ambush after another. One day you ambush them, the next maybe they ambush you." In the ambush of a full company, you wanted to let the first targets, the scouts, go by without firing. You wanted to wait until the middle of the line was passing or even wait for the last men because that is where the officers—if there were any—would most likely be and also where you would find the men carrying the radio, machine gun and the mortar if they had one. You wanted to kill the officers and capture those pieces.

Our unit commander, Candido, was right in the middle of our ambush line and he would wait for the right moment and fire first. Everyone would wait for that and then open up. You started with your weapon on automatic to fire a long burst, so that in the initial surprise, when they would freeze for moments, you would kill as many as possible.

About a half hour after the sun came up, an old campesino man in white pants and a beat-up straw hat walked down the trail leading a couple of horses, probably taking them to graze. He didn't know we were there, although at one point he looked right up in the direction where we were dug in, as if he sensed us. But he kept going. When he first came into view I had him in the sights of my rifle and I got another taste of what was coming, what it would be like to kill someone. As Candido said, "They never know what hits them."

About an hour after dawn, they came down the trail. The first of them was very young, very dark, very short, dressed in fatigues, but wearing his rifle over his shoulder as if he were out for a stroll and in no danger. Then came another and another, all of them close together, which is against the rules they'd taught me in San José. You never walked close to one another because one burst of automatic weapon fire or one grenade could take out a bunch of you. That way you made it easy for your enemy.

They walked right under the sight of my assault rifle. Then I saw two of them with machine guns over their shoulders come into view. Candido was dug in farther down the trail. I let them pass, but when they reached him, he opened up and then so did I and everyone else. The sound was deafening. The flat metallic clacking of ten assault rifles filling the ravine. There was an older *guardia* directly below me, right in the sights of my rifle when it started. He had a thick moustache that was turning grey. I saw the surprise on his face, his eyes round, his mouth open, and I saw his body jump as the bullets hit him. Ever since then that's how death looks to me, that surprise.

The shooting lasted less than a minute. First we all opened up on automatic. I saw the several *guardia* on my stretch of the trail fall. Apparently one of their machine gunners was only injured, or not hit at all, and managed to throw himself down into the ravine and open up on us. Bullets began to whiz overhead, cutting through the vegetation and sprinkling pieces of it down on me. I felt like meat being seasoned. Then our backup, five other guerrillas farther up the hill, started firing to cover our retreat. We made it over the crest of the hill, where we were safe from their fire. They wouldn't be chasing us, they would be seeing to their wounded.

We made double time back in the direction we'd come. There was a terrible sound that I'd been hearing for a while. It was the monkeys in the trees, scared out of their wits by the firing, and they were howling.

We got back to the camp quickly, much more quickly than it had taken to get to the ambush spot. It was as if the mountains changed size, became easier to maneuver when you survived an encounter with the enemy. When we got back to the camp everyone was happy. Candido estimated we'd killed at least twenty of them.

I didn't get into the celebration. I still had the sound of the shooting in my head. I thought of what Mena had said: "Guerrilla war is one ambush after another." Some day it would be your turn to be in the sights of a rifle. Also, I hadn't been in the mountains long enough to know that you should celebrate your victories. In guerrilla war, they're often few and far between.

Lavinia was also quiet. We got our food and for the first time began to talk. She asked me about the United States, she'd never been there. She also asked me if I had a wife or a girlfriend. I told her I had just recently gotten divorced.

The unit stayed put the next two days. The night of that second day Lavinia and I became lovers. We found a spot off in bushes away from the others and we were quiet. It was like sneaking off to the park back in New York.

The next day the unit moved to another section of the sierra ten kilometers away and we began political work there, making contact with collaborators we already had, recruiting new ones, giving people the message. I didn't participate because I wasn't Nicaraguan, but I listened and I posted guard. At one point we saw government planes in the sky, reconnaissance flights, but the terrain was too wooded for them to see us.

Over the next few months I became a fair guerrilla. Some people develop their abilities for that kind of life more easily than others. Me, I guess growing up in a neighborhood where you always had to watch yourself, that taught me a thing or two. During that time, we pulled off more ambushes and attacked one small guard garrison in a village. We charged the place. I might as well have been drunk or stoned for all I can remember of it. It was like running right at death.

It was in that attack that Carlos was killed. He took a bullet in the chest. We managed to drag him away and he died that day with his head lying in my hands. It was the first time I'd ever had a friend killed. We wrapped his body in a poncho and buried him where we could find him later when the war was over. If it was ever over.

It was when Carlos was killed that the whole thing changed for me. Before then it had been, more than anything, an adventure. After he got killed and I helped bury him, the fight became something I had to finish. I had to get revenge.

A month later, the final push came. We made up part of the battalion that was ordered to attack the provincial capital of Jinotega. For the next few nights I didn't sleep. The adrenaline kept me awake. The dream was either going to come true or die. The guys we met up with had mortars, machine guns, old, but still usable. We were given grenades, a couple of sniper rifles, grenade launchers. For us it was like going from the American Revolution to Vietnam.

She and I were assigned to different units for the assault on the city. That was Candido's work. He

didn't want us watching each other, trying to protect
each other and not doing our jobs. We had developed
a kind of clandestine relationship. The others knew
about it, but we didn't talk much to each other when
the others were around. We had fallen for each other
fast and hard. Maybe it was the fact we could be killed
at any time, but it was also her. She was a guerrilla
and did her job in the hills, but when we were alone
she lost that edge. She was a woman. Maybe she loved
me to save herself from getting too hard, from letting
fear and killing become too much a part of her. Maybe
loving her saved me from that too. After the war, she
said, we would live in Managua. That was it. It was
an order.

The attack on Jinotega was to be our last dangerous
action. The whole country would fall soon. It started
with a mortar attack on the *guardia* garrison. She died
in the original incursion, but I didn't know it until the
next day. The guys in her unit had her body in the
church. It was wrapped in her poncho and lying in
front of the altar. I didn't look at her.

We took Jinotega, and Managua fell the next day.
Victor Mena found me there a week after the fighting
ended. He knew what had happened, after all he was
intelligence. He told me I should stay in Nicaragua. I
spent about a month there, but I couldn't get comfortable. It wasn't the way I'd planned it with her. I
told Mena I was getting out and he tried to talk me
out of it. I didn't listen.

I headed back to San José to pick up my stuff I'd
left there. I stayed drunk for a week or two. When I
sobered up, I bumped into an old Costa Rican man
I'd met there before, who made me the offer to run
his club. It was called The Tropical. He said with the
fighting over now up in Nicaragua, tourism would

pick up and it would be good to have an American partner, especially one who knew something about the bar and restaurant business. In time I could buy him out. It was an offer I couldn't refuse.

I never went back to New York, except to visit. Now nine years later, people were showing up to remind me all about the Nicaragua days. Like that was what I needed.

Chapter
—5—

THE next morning the papers still had the bombing story all over the front page.

The journalists had found out a few more things about Topo's movements during his last days. He'd flown into the country on a Costa Rican airlines flight from Nicaragua just three days before, using his real name. But then he had checked into a hotel, a small place right in the center of the city, under an alias. The manager there identified an old police photo. He had moved out of the hotel after one day and it wasn't known where he had stayed his last two nights alive.

Reporters interviewed the Nicaraguan ambassador to ask him about the flight from Managua, but he said neither he nor anyone else in his government had contact with Morales in recent years. He "absolutely denied" any connection between his government and the bombing.

A bunch of Costa Rican politicians were interviewed who suggested they didn't believe the Nicaraguan ambassador. They all made statements, some more direct than others, in which they implied the Sandinistas had killed Topo, a man known to have been a Sandinista agent in the past. One of the politicians, named Corvo, a young bull in the ruling party who was mentioned as a future presidential candidate, said he thought the Sandinistas were settling accounts amongst themselves but using Costa Rican territory to do it and risking setting off a regional war. "We only have to look across our northern border to know who did this," he said.

And there was Pepe Esparza, the Dessert Man, who got his chubby face in the papers saying that the Sandinistas were threatening Costa Rican nationals and the country's democratic system and they should be overthrown.

In another article, Major Eddie Pasos said the police had established the bomb was remote controlled. That explained why the prostitutes across from the club had not seen anyone actually plant the device. He said an autopsy showed Topo Morales had died of wounds from the blast.

Meanwhile, I told Jacoba, my housekeeper, to keep the phone off the hook. I had just been getting into bed the night before, when the phone had rung, some reporter from Miami. Somehow my home number had gotten out. I finished with him and then it was another from some British paper and then a third one from a Portuguese weekly. Finally I'd just taken it off the hook. First of all I didn't know anything more than the papers had already carried, at least not more that I was going to tell them. I wasn't about to give them any kind of scoop. And second, when you're a foreigner doing business in a country you want to stay out of any international incidents. I also told Jacoba not to let anybody in she didn't know, that I was unavailable.

I read the papers in the hammock next to the garden. My parrot, Ollie, was in his cage, inching back and forth on his wooden bar and squawking. Conchita, the spider monkey who lived in the eucalyptus tree, was working on a mango.

When I finished the news I laid back and looked out at the countryside and, in the distance, the city. In the spring, before the rains, the farmers would set fire to the hillsides to prepare them for planting and the valley would fill with a smoky haze. They called it the "burn season." In Nicaragua it was the same, and during the insurrection, there were days we had used that haze to cover our movements. But once the rains came they washed haze away and you could see and be seen.

Now the mountainside was lush and green from heavy rains. Just down the slope from my place there was a family that planted a large field of corn. It was shoulder high now, but still green. I walked down through there from time to time even though the going was muddy and the traction difficult. I'd walk all along the side of the mountain until it dipped into a culvert where a stream ran by and banana trees were growing. Then I'd take a trail up towards the ridge and from there you could see San José in one direction and in the other, the mountains rolling to the south.

Sometimes I'd doze off in the hammock and I'd dream about New York. I'd hear the traffic, the subways, I'd be surrounded by the tall glass buildings, the crowds on the sidewalks, get that feeling of a city all around me. Then I'd wake up and be looking at this tropical mountain and I wouldn't know where I was. I'd hear Spanish and it would sound like a language I didn't know. When you lived in a country that wasn't your own, you lost it sometimes. Especially in my case, where my life had changed almost overnight. It always seemed to me like it might change again at any time, that anything could happen.

I was dozing off right then, when I heard the doorbell ring. I heard Jacoba answer it and tell someone that I was asleep and unavailable. She was combative, old Jacoba, she'd protect me. The person talked a bit more, a woman it was, but Jacoba stood firm. The door closed and I shut my eyes again. A minute later I was almost asleep, when I heard a woman's voice right above me.

"Mr. Lacey?"

I opened my eyes and she was standing next to the hammock. She must have come through the bushes on the side of the house and then across the patio and I hadn't heard her. She looked tall from where I was lying, but even if I hadn't been lying down she was tall. She had very light skin and very dark hair and eyes. She was dressed in a green jumpsuit with a red sash at the waist and she was carrying a briefcase. She was perfectly collected, which was more than I could say for myself. I just stared at her from the hammock.

"My name is Lucia Lara. I am a political counselor at the Nicaraguan embassy here in San José," she said in lightly accented English. "I would like to question you about the incident at your club the other evening."

She said all this as if she had come through the front door with an appointment and not snuck into my house. This in itself was a trick. She also made it sound like she was there to interrogate me, but I think it was just a peculiarity of her English. Anyway, worse things could happen to you than to be interrogated by a woman who looked like she did.

"Do you always sneak into people's houses this way?"

She took it seriously.

"No, I don't, but my ambassador thought you would rather talk here out of the way, than at your club where people might tell stories." Her dark eyes narrowed. "We represent the Nicaraguan government and we are not popular in Costa Rica these days. That was his thinking."

"Yes, I've just been reading the reviews," I told her, and I tapped the papers.

It was true what she said, it would be better not to be seen talking to her in the middle of a crowded bar. The question was whether I should talk to her at all. I'd taken the phone off the hook, so I couldn't deal with her that way. Now she'd gotten the drop on me, and then there was the way she looked. I asked her to sit down, and called Jacoba, who gave my backdoor visitor a dirty look, and then went to get us something to drink.

I settled back in the hammock.

"Well, if you're here to interrogate me, I'll tell you one thing: I didn't plant that bomb. If I did I would have done it someplace else."

She nodded.

"We assumed it was not yourself. You don't have a history as a saboteur."

"Do you know who did do it?"

She shook her head.

"Not for sure. All we know is that our government wasn't involved, although we are being accused." She got a sardonic glint in her eye. "Since we were guerrillas once, when a bomb goes off we are the prime suspects. I think you understand."

I didn't say anything to that. Jacoba came back then with a pitcher of papaya juice and served us. Ollie was chattering away in his cage, although he hadn't made a sound as she'd snuck up on me. Conchita was jumping from branch to branch and jabbering.

My visitor watched Jacoba leave and looked around at the place. It was all varnished hardwood beams, red tile floor and garden.

"Your house is very rustic and very out of the way," she said.

"It's a good place to hide, although maybe not good enough." I smiled when I said it and she just looked at me knowingly. She had a way of looking at you from behind a wave of black hair, a suspicious look, as if she were watching you from behind a tree.

Then she leaned back in the chair and became all business.

"I have come here because we are in a propaganda war, Mr. Lacey, and we will have to defend ourselves from attacks being made against us because of this recent bombing. It would be helpful to know exactly what this man Morales said to you before he died. We have read what the authorities are saying, but sometimes they withhold information."

So I said what the hell and I laid back in the hammock and told it all again. What the dead man had said to me, just like I'd told it to Eddie and the Dessert Man. I probably should have made a tape recording of it just to save myself time. She listened to what I said very carefully. I told her the same story until I got to Topo's mentioning of Victor Mena. And then I stepped off the trail.

I was thinking about it as I was talking. If I told her something I hadn't told the government and it got out, I was in a spot. But then it wouldn't get out, because she wouldn't want Mena's name attached to Topo's killing. And then there was the outside chance that Topo really had been on an operation for the Sandinistas, and I wanted her and her bosses at the embassy to know that I didn't like "old war buddies" sneaking out of my past and getting me involved in their bombings.

So I said to her: "There was one other thing. He told me Victor Mena from Nicaraguan state security sent him."

I watched her as I said it and I saw surprise in her face. It passed quickly. She sat dead still for several moments, staring at me, as if she were searching for the lie in my eyes, just like Topo had. It was the guerrilla experience, I assume. It left people forever suspicious.

"You *do* know Victor Mena, don't you?" I said.

She nodded abstractedly.

"I know who he is," she said and searched my gaze some more. "Morales told you that, but you know it wasn't true. He made it up."

Her voice was steady, not excited, but I knew I'd touched a nerve. In her eyes, there was a glint now, sharp and wary.

I shrugged.

"I didn't think it was true, but you never know. I thought Victor might be organizing cells again."

She shook her head and watched me from behind her tree.

"There's absolutely no truth in what he said. Mo-

69

rales was once a collaborator of ours, but not any longer. I know he was not involved in any operation for us. I can assure you of it."

It was my turn to search her eyes. They were beautiful eyes, dark brown with green highlights. Their gaze was cool, suspicious. Behind them, however, you sensed something different, more passionate, that was being kept under control. At least at the moment there seemed to be nothing dishonest hiding in them. She let me stare into them for a while to make sure. After a few seconds I wasn't worried about whether she was telling the truth, I was just getting lost in her eyes. Finally, Ollie squawked and broke the quiet. I got up to refill my glass from the pitcher on the bar.

"Like I told you, I didn't really believe him," I said. "I thought he was trying to sucker me into something, but that isn't why I wouldn't help him."

She was following me as if she were tracking me through a rifle sight.

"Why didn't you?"

I leaned with my back against the bar.

"I wouldn't have helped him even if Victor Mena had sent him on a mission," I said. "I want you to know it and anybody else who might be interested. I'm not involved in those games anymore. I came out of the sierra a long time ago. I hope you understand that?"

She tilted her head and gave me a sidelong look.

"Then why didn't you tell the Costa Rican authorities what Morales said to you about Victor Mena? You knew that sort of information would be harmful to us. Why did you withhold it?"

"I didn't tell them only because I didn't want my name connected with Mena or any other Sandinista guerrilla leader. Believe me, I wasn't covering for you, I was covering for myself."

She drank that in as if it tasted bitter.

"I understand," she said.

"I hope so."

She crossed her legs and stayed staring down at her dark red high-heel shoe, swiveling it as if she was reading something written there.

"Much information will come out now about Morales's past service with us as an intelligence agent," she said. "It will be used to accuse us of his death and of inviting war with Costa Rica."

"It's already being used."

She looked up at me.

"It is true that Morales worked for us at one time, but we always knew he wasn't one of us, that he was not to be trusted. He was the son of a wealthy cattle rancher in the southern part of our country near the Costa Rican border and his mother was from Costa Rica. The family had a lot of money, had nothing really to gain from our revolution and the father was always against us."

"But Topo did work with you and I heard he was a good undercover man," I said.

"Yes, he joined us. And it is true that he was for a time a very valuable intelligence agent on the southern front. He was a spy. He brought us information on the troop movements of Somoza's National Guard, on the number and kind of armaments they had. Because of his family's political ties to Somoza, he was never suspected. But he was no idealist and no revolutionary. He was a mercenary. He realized that Somoza could not resist us and it would be best to be on the winning side."

"Sounds like Topo," I said.

"After the insurrection, much of his father's family left Nicaragua as did many of the other collaborators of Somoza. We invited Morales to work for us, and he did for a time."

"In state security," I said, "with Victor Mena."

"But only for a short time," she insisted. "He realized he would not get rich working for us and he left. I understand he came back to Costa Rica and was involved in criminal activities."

"I understand he was involved as an informant for various intelligence organizations, including yours," I said.

Her dark eyes narrowed.

"That is not true."

Just then Conchita swung down to a lower branch and began chattering.

"Not even the monkey believes that."

"I'm not lying," she said.

I laid down in the hammock again, arms behind my head.

"And you wouldn't lie, would you? Not even for your cause."

She was back behind her tree again watching me.

"Of course I would and I have."

She looked me in the eyes to tell me that. Just like Topo had his crook's mentality, she had her guerrilla morality. She looked you straight in the eye to tell you she was capable of lying for the cause. The code of the outlaw.

"Where were you during the insurrection?" I asked her. "To have a job as important as yours, you must have put in years of service before the last push in seventy-nine."

She thought, as if she were deciding whether or not I was worthy of that information. I guess I was.

"I was in the city of León," she said.

"Fighting?"

"I joined the *Frente* in nineteen seventy-five and first I was a recruiter at the university. Then we were infiltrated and I had to go underground. I worked clandestinely for two years. When the fighting began in León in nineteen seventy-nine I was part of the force that took the city. It fell ten days before Managua."

She had her long legs crossed, bright red fingernails rested on her knee and she looked nothing like a guerrilla.

"Did you ever kill anybody in that fighting?"

She looked at me curiously.

"Of course, it was a war."

"It's still a war," I said. "Ask Topo."

She shot me a nasty look.

"I told you no one from my government had anything to do with this killing."

"You can speak for yourself and maybe I believe you," I said, "but you were in a guerrilla organization long enough to know that there are always things you aren't told. You know as much as you need to, and you can never be sure what someone else in the organization is up to."

Now the amusement disappeared from her eyes. She knew what I was saying was true and she didn't like it. I said to her:

"But let's suppose it wasn't the Sandinistas who killed Topo. Who was it?"

She fingered her glass.

"We don't know for sure, but we believe it was the Contras."

"Of course," I said. "Who else? They accuse you, you accuse them."

She shook her head so that her shiny black hair swung back and forth.

"It's more than that," she said. "We know he had been dealing with the Contras lately."

"Then why was he in Managua just five days ago? He flew from there to here."

"His name was not on the prohibited list. He could enter the country at any time," she said. "We don't know what he was doing there."

"Maybe he was visiting his dear old grandmother."

"We have checked with those members of his family who are still there," she said. "They say they have not seen him in some time. They weren't even sure he was alive."

"Well, at least they won't miss him." I sipped my juice. "Or maybe he was in Managua on an assignment for his new Contra bosses and that's why you had reason to get rid of him."

She shook me off.

"We don't know why they killed him. In clandestine organizations people turn against each other. There is often infighting," she said.

"Well, I guess you people would know."

I said that with a smile. She didn't return it.

"You've gotten serious," I said.

She clenched her jaws before she spoke.

"This is a very serious matter, Mr. Lacey. Our country is going through a war and is threatened by a larger war."

I stayed looking at her but didn't answer. Because now she reminded me of somebody, somebody dead. It had been there all along, but now with the serious tone, the steady eye, the resemblance was clear.

Somewhere down the hill, there was a shot. Probably the local farmer shooting at the crows trying to eat his green corn. It didn't attract her attention at all. She had probably heard enough shooting in her time to know when it mattered. She was watching me like somebody she thought she recognized but wasn't sure.

"I'm told that you yourself were a good guerrilla," she said finally. "That during the insurrection you served the cause courageously. It is curious how a man could change so much. To act now as if he doesn't care. I wonder if that is true."

I shook my head sadly.

"It's true all right," I said. "I've fallen into the trap of bourgeois, capitalist pleasures. Drinking, dancing, gambling et cetera. I'm telling you the truth."

I looked her straight in the eyes as I made my confession. If she could look me in the eye to say she was a liar I could do the same to tell her I was dissolute. She returned the stare a few moments, as if she was looking for somebody else inside me. If this was an attempt to recruit me, it wasn't going anywhere. After a while I guess she thought the same. She couldn't find that other person.

She put aside the drink, brought the briefcase to her lap, snapped open the locks, lifted the lid, and stuck her hand inside. Then I was absolutely sure this cool, pale young woman was going to pull a pistol out of there, stand up, take aim and empty it into me. Maybe because of the way she had snuck into the house, maybe because of her saying, "We used to be guerrillas," maybe because she told me she had killed before. Or maybe it was that Topo really had mentioned Victor Mena to me, and I was the only one alive who knew that.

All those reasons, plus the fact I hadn't asked for identification and I didn't know who she really was and what she was there to do. So my breath got caught for a moment as her hand disappeared into the brief-

75

case. She pulled it out and reached towards me, but what was in her hand was a card. I took it from her. It said Lucia Lara, Nicaraguan embassy, and it had numbers.

"You can reach me there if there is need," she said. I breathed again and nodded at her.

She snapped the briefcase closed, stood up, and so did I.

"You can leave through the door if you would like," I said. "Or you can sneak out through the garden if you'd rather."

We stopped at the door. I told her she should come by the club and catch the floor show some night soon and she said she would. We shook hands then.

"I'd like to thank you for your time and your help," she said.

"I haven't given you any help," I said pointedly. "And please don't tell anyone I have."

She looked at me for a second from behind that tree of hers. Then I watched her go to her car and drive away.

Chapter

— 6 —

FRIDAY and Saturday were my big nights. The floor show with Isla Vega and her Caribbean Current always pulled them in.

Isla was a Puerto Rican girl who fronted a ten-piece band and a small chorus line. She had toured all over the Caribbean, played Miami and once worked on the cruise ships that sailed out of there. But she had gotten sick of the sea. "During the day all you does is look at the goddam water," she said. So she went back to Puerto Rico and worked the casinos, and then later to Venezuela. She was playing in Grenada at the time of the U.S. invasion there. "I like soldiers, baby, but not when they are shooting people."

Then she'd gone to the Dominican Republic. In the D.R. she'd gotten involved with a trumpet player— or two, actually—and there had been a blowup. One had ended up dead and Isla put out to sea again. She led a stormy life, Isla. Finally, she'd washed up in San

77

José and hooked up these boys from the Caribbean Current, which had turned out good for her and for me too. The past three months she'd been headlining at The Tropical.

Isla had legs on her as long as palm trees and more teeth in her smile than a barracuda. She sang in Spanish and English and danced up a storm. She was breezy when she wanted to be and hot too. She called herself the Puerto Rican Hurricane. I was prejudiced, but I thought she was good enough for Las Vegas, Havana or anyplace else for that matter.

It rained like hell that afternoon. I was worried the streets might flood and then with bombs going off in my parking lot and the newspapers talking about the tide of violence in Central America, I didn't know how we'd do. As it turned out I shouldn't have worried. Maybe people wanted to see where it had all happened, I don't know, but the floor show was at midnight and by 11:30 the place was almost full. Not quite the usual crowd, some locals had stayed away, but not bad. Couples moved around the dance floor. The women were dressed to kill, lots of bare shoulders and jewelry. The waiters in their bright white shirts were weaving quickly between the tables with their trays above their heads. The bar was busy and the old Chinamen in the casino had some company tonight.

One of the other players in the casino was the American pilot, Chelly. He was sitting at the blackjack table and I asked him how he was doing.

"So far friendly skies, Jack. I'm a little up."

"Well, you've always been a lucky boy, Chelly," I told him.

"Yes, I have," he said, and his blue eyes lighted up happily. "Lately I've been especially lucky."

"Is that right? What have you been carrying lately, Contra nurses?"

He grinned and shook his head.

"No, Jack. I've been carrying air, planeloads of air."

I looked at him. He wasn't making much sense but he obviously thought this was very funny. He was probably very stoned.

"Well, at least it doesn't weigh much," I said. "It won't drag you down."

"It don't weigh anything, and they pay me to move it from one place to another."

I didn't know what he was talking about, but I said: "Must be good air."

He laughed his spaced-out laugh and I glanced out into the club. "That's a nice crowd you have out there," he said.

"Yeah, and I better go out and take care of it," I said. I wished him luck and went back out.

Ray Reed was working the door, getting people to their tables. The worst problem you had on a night like this when the dance floor got crowded was drunks, guys with too much rum in them. Fights kicked up on the dance floor like sudden squalls. That's where Ray came in. One look at the size of him and that steel hook which he always kept shined and the drunks sobered up fast. If they didn't, they'd go out of there like fish, on the end of that hook.

I stopped to see how things were going.

"Smooth sailing so far, boss," Ray said.

So I went and sat at my table in the alcove near the office and checked out the crowd. There were a few tables of Costa Ricans. At a couple of tables you had government officials who I recognized. They were wining and dining some Japanese gentlemen, who I

79

assumed were potential investors in the country. Of course, because of the wars in Central America, no one was investing much these days, but it went on the expense account and everybody had a nice time. They were at ringside just across from me. Next to them, on one side was Frank Quintero, a Panamanian diplomat I knew, and he had a bunch of people with him.

Frank had been one of the top soccer players with the Panamanian national team, a figure in his country. He was a smart boy as well. He had retired young after an injury and had gone into the foreign service of his government, using contacts he had all over Central America to help his career. Everybody knew Frank and Frank knew everybody. He had the same dark curly hair and flashing smile he'd had as a player and the same slim-waisted athletic build.

They said as a diplomat he was the same as he had been as a soccer player too, fast on his feet. In Central America it was said that the Panamanians did legitimate business with everybody and illegitimate business with everybody as well. They were true democrats. It was said that they sold arms to both left and right. They had contacts with both the U.S. and Castro, with both the Colombian drug dealers and the U.S. Drug Enforcement people. They were highly social, the Panamanians, especially Frank. He gave me a smile and wave.

Next to Frank there was a table of Colombians I didn't know. I could tell they were Colombians because they had more emeralds on than you found in the Tower of London. The next table was full of Cubans. Or they used to be Cubans before they left because they didn't want to share the island with Castro.

Or Castro didn't want to share it with them. Now they lived in Costa Rica, making rum, maybe growing a bit of tobacco and doing other business.

The next table was full of Honduran military officers dressed in civvies, with some women who were uniformly younger than them and looked Costa Rican. Maybe they were prostitutes, but if they were with escorts I had no beef. The Hondurans were down on R and R and I wasn't going to interfere with their good time. Some of these officers were leaning over talking to the people at the next table. That was Pepe Esparza and some of his Contra buddies. They had a working relationship, the Hondurans and the Contras, which was maybe what they were talking about. I didn't want to know.

The rest of the place was full with who knows who. I saw a table of European diplomats and some tourists. Then about five minutes before the floor show was supposed to begin, Lucia Lara walked in. She was wearing a tight black dress with bare shoulders. There were two guys with her in white *guayabera* shirts, who I assumed were also from the Nicaraguan embassy. She stopped and looked around. She met my eyes for part of a second, but didn't make a show of it. Ray met them and led them across the dance floor to a table just off ringside.

I looked over at Pepe Esparza where he was sitting between the Hondurans and the Cubans. His glass stopped in mid-drink and his smile dried up. He nudged one of his buddies next to him and they all tracked Ms. Lara and her escorts as they crossed the floor. Other people in the place, the diplomats, the government officials, had also noticed the Sandinista delegation. You saw the heads turn and the crowd noise suddenly got lower. She walked right through it all as if she hadn't noticed. But there were some restless souls in the crowd and that wasn't good.

I went over and told the boys in the band to crank it up and get the show going. They went into a big brassy salsa number and that got everyone's attention. I figured the sooner I got Isla out on the floor the better. I'd use my own hurricane before another one kicked up on its own.

Ray hit the switches and the overhead spot threw a pool of moonlight on the dance floor. The band played a short intro and then Isla walked into the light. She was wearing a blue costume studded with rhinestones, a costume that didn't cover any of her long legs or beautiful brown shoulders or the tops of her breasts. She wore this headdress made of rhinestones too, and every time she moved, the light played on the stones and on her eyes which were just as bright. She was like a comet over the Caribbean. She was good, Isla. From the second she walked out there, she had them surrounded.

She went into her first number, a fiery song about a girl from the islands. And now everybody in the place was watching her. Except for Pepe Esparza, that is. I saw him still gazing across the floor towards that other table.

I went over to see Ray on the other side of the floor.

"Keep an eye out," I told him. "I can feel trouble brewing."

Ray nodded, eyes on the floor.

"Stormy weather on the horizon," he said.

Isla had three girls dancing behind her. A tall, sleek-bodied girl named Coco; Rita Sierra, who was dark and large in the chest and hips, and then a light-skinned girl named Carmen. Something for everybody. Isla did a version of "All Night Long" for the gringos while the girls did a quick costume change. The costumes got skimpier as the songs got hotter. They did reggae, some calypso banana boat stuff, a Haitian voodoo ballad, and they finished up with a long salsa number, a hip-grinding affair that had the place shaking. Isla did an encore, a steamy bolero, and it took about two minutes for the applause to die altogether. Then the band swung into some dance music and the floor began to fill up. At that point, everything was smooth sailing.

Frankie Quintero, the Panamanian diplomat, came over and sat down with me.

"That Isla she's very hot," he said with a mischievous grin. "You are not helping her change her costumes, are you, Jack?"

I shook my head.

"She's too hot for me, Frankie," I told him. "Anyway, I don't play the trumpet. She likes trumpet players."

"I don't play either," he said. He shrugged and looked around. "This crowd you have here tonight, it is very interesting."

"I wish it weren't so interesting," I said.

Frankie glanced across the room.

"Miss Lara from the Nicaraguan embassy, she caused some waves when she came in. Some people here didn't like it."

She was sitting with her two escorts. People were still glancing over at them and the two men were looking around cautiously. She, on the other hand, sat watching the dancing, perfectly calm at the eye of the whirlpool.

"Miss Lara would cause waves anywhere," I said. "Do you know her?"

Frankie considered the question, as if he were looking for an angle for a soccer kick.

"I know her from the diplomatic receptions," he said, "and I know what people say about her."

"Which is?"

"That she is a woman of some experience," he said suggestively. "That she is a person, as we say in Spanish, *de cuidado*. You should be careful with her."

"Because she fought in the insurrection?"

"They say two things about her. That back in the seventies she had lovers who are now amongst the most powerful men in Nicaragua." He shrugged. "But of course, back then the Sandinista Front was a small clandestine organization and people could only really know each other and trust each other, no outsiders. It was natural that they take each other for lovers."

"What else do they say about her?"

"That before the Sandinista victory she spent several years underground. That she was involved in smuggling guns, money, false documents from country to country and finally to the Sandinistas. That she also gathered information all over Central America for the Sandinista Front. Of course, with the way she looks you can understand why men might tell her things."

"So she was a spy and you think she still is."

Frankie made a face.

"Don't be indiscreet, Jack. Your language is too explicit. Anyway, all we diplomats are spies to a degree, aren't we? We are all gathering information for our governments."

"But she's doing a particularly good job of it. Is that it?"

Frankie shrugged and sipped his drink. Out on the floor people were dancing a merengue.

I asked him, "Have you gathered any information on who killed Topo Morales?"

Frankie and the other Panamanians at their embassy, with all their tricky business around Central America, had sources everywhere. Frankie considered the question.

"It's hard to tell. Morales was mixed up with everyone."

"It's almost as if he was from Panama," I said.

Frankie smiled and gazed at the crowd.

"I've heard probably the same things you have heard," he said. "Topo was mixed up with the Contras, the Costa Rican security forces, the Sandinistas, with smugglers and other criminals. Some people say he even had dealings with the CIA. But I've also heard that lately there have been in Costa Rica some Colombian and some Cuban gentlemen who are involved in this smuggling business. Some especially important Colombian gentlemen."

"Who are these gentlemen?"

"I'm not sure who, but I know that they flew up here from Medellín city."

Frankie watched for my reaction and he wasn't disappointed. It caught my attention. The Medellín boys were the biggest cocaine smugglers in the world.

"Do you really think Topo could have been playing in that league?"

Frankie shrugged.

"I'm just telling you what I know, Jack. I don't know who killed Topo. I just think the timing it is interesting."

He sipped his drink and looked out over the crowd. Then he said:

"Have you ever heard of a man named Cassanova, Raul Cassanova?"

I pulled a face.

"No, I haven't."

Frankie glanced across the floor.

"At the table with the Colombians," he said. "The man dressed in white."

I looked over and saw a small man, extremely tanned with thinning black hair, wearing a white suit that looked very expensive. He was smiling broadly and showed teeth that looked like they went with the suit, white and expensive.

"Who is he?"

Frankie shook his head as if it were no big deal.

"A businessman from Miami. They say he is here to do some investing."

I waited for him to say more but he didn't. His attention was drawn away from me to the dance floor. I saw why. Lucia Lara had taken to the floor and was being steered around by one of her escorts. She was a half head taller than him and taller than any other woman on the floor. They were dancing a merengue, and while her bare shoulders shook with the rhythm, her face floated above the crowd.

"She is something," Frankie said.

I didn't have a chance to answer. I was watching her when the next thing I see is a big guy in a red shirt, one of Pepe Esparza's boys, with a woman in his arms, heading across the dance floor right towards her, like a shark. Then he crashes right into the guy she's dancing with. You could see it coming. There was the collision, bad looks exchanged, words, and the next thing you know this same jerk is throwing a roundhouse punch. A couple of women scream, and people are scattering. I look for Ray and I see he's already on the dance floor heading towards them. By the time I get there he and Chico and some of the other waiters are between them. Ray has his hook in the belt of the guy in the red shirt.

"Get him out of here," I tell him, and Ray begins to drag the guy out.

Then Pepe Esparza is at my elbow and yelling something about "communists." I turn on him and get right up in his face.

"Don't bring your politics into my place. Cut it out or I'll throw you out too."

Pepe stops yelling and sneers at me.

"Now we know whose side you on."

"I'm not on anybody's side. I'm on my side." I jab a finger into his fat chest. "I don't want this crap in my club."

Pepe stands there a few seconds more, glaring at me, his fat shaking with anger and his face a deep red. I can feel the other sharks all around waiting for him to attack so that they can all feed on me. But finally Pepe just makes a sound of disgust in his phlegmy throat, turns around and stalks away. The others begin to draw back.

I motion to the band and they begin playing again. I notice her then. She's been standing right in the middle of it, not moving, the calm at the eye of the storm. I looked at her, she met my gaze for a moment and then I walked away.

Frankie Quintero was standing next to my table, and he raised his glass in a toast.

"Here's to neutrality," he said. "You spoke like a true Costa Rican patriot."

I took a deep drink from my *mojito* and kept an eye on things. The place was buzzing. People were shooting looks over at the table where Lucia Lara sat as still and cool as the moon.

I went to the door to see Ray. Together we watched

87

the guy in the red shirt and a couple of his buddies get in their car and drive away.

"Those guys they'll never wash up here again," Ray said.

We were still there, taking the air, when Lucia Lara and her friends came out. We met on the steps.

"Leaving so early?" I said to her.

One of her escorts put a jacket over her bare shoulders.

"I'm sorry about the turbulence," she said in her English, "but we did nothing to provoke it."

I had to smile then. She was enough to provoke anybody. She was watching my eyes and a smile played at the corners of her mouth as if she knew what I was thinking.

"It wasn't your doing," I said. "Those guys were looking for trouble. You and your friends are free to come back anytime."

"Thank you," she said. "I'll come back." We shook hands then. She had that same smile in her eyes, as if we were playing at something for the benefit of witnesses. Or as if she knew something I didn't. She held my hand an extra moment more than necessary and then she left.

We watched them cross the lot.

"Watch out, boss," Ray said. "Small craft warnings there."

He laughed and then we went back inside.

The buzzing had stopped, people were on the dance floor and things were back to normal. The stormy weather was over. Isla had come out to watch this other show and now, with a dressing gown over her costume, she slipped over to the table.

"I think you have a new girlfriend, Jack," she said.

Her black eyes were full of mischief. "I think you like her. You have a thing for the Nicaraguan womens."

I leaned over and gave her a kiss on her rouged cheek.

Isla had a thing for me. But I had heard from her about how she'd broken up with her trumpet players over the years. I decided I didn't want to lose her and her show and I didn't want to have to rebuild my club from splinters. So I let the opportunity pass. Isla had a Costa Rican coffee planter for a boyfriend now and sometimes I saw her with Chelly, the pilot. Still, I heard a strain of jealousy in her lovely voice.

"I don't know the woman," I said.

Isla looked at me with a sly smile that said she knew better.

"If you don't knows her, you are going to knows her, Jack." She winked at me, gave me a peck on the cheek and went out.

The rest of the night went smoothly, at least until I headed home.

The last customers left at 4:30 and I was out of there by 5. I drove in the last of the dark. It had rained on and off all night, the roads were still wet, the streetlights were far apart and I went easy on the curves leading up to the house.

A few hundred yards from my place I made a sharp curve in the road that led into a climbing straight-away. The vegetation on the hillside was thick and tropical and you could smell it and the rain. As I came out of the turn I heard this noise, like exploding firecrackers, maybe a half dozen pops. I didn't know what the hell it was. Then from the bushes on the side of the road straight ahead of me I saw the muzzle flashes, another half dozen shots. Somebody was shooting at me.

I stamped the brakes, felt the car go into a slide, turned the wheel away from the ditch on the left, went into a spin and saw the mountain go all the way around the car, until finally I went into the soft shoulder and rammed the hillside. More shots sounded and I jammed it into reverse and tried to get back around the curve, but the wheels just spun in the mud making a screaming sound. I killed the lights, dived facedown on the passenger seat and waited for the windshield to explode above me. Getting out would only give them a clear shot at me.

But nothing burst. I laid there and waited. Then I heard a door slam and a car take off. I looked up in time to see the red taillights turning off on a fork that went back down the hillside.

After a minute I got out and checked the jeep. There wasn't a hole in it. Not one. The shots had all gone over me. I walked up the road slowly and stopped where I saw the spent shells on the shoulder behind a bush. Automatic rifle ammunition; 7.62 mm, the same kind I'd used in the Nicaraguan sierra. I picked one up and it was still warm. I looked around, but there was nothing or nobody else. I put it in my pocket for good luck; my good luck that whoever it was hadn't wanted to kill me, only to scare me.

I put a rock in the mud under the wheel and got the car free. Then I turned onto the short dirt road that led to my place and drove the last few hundred meters slowly. Jacoba went home to her own house at night so I didn't have to worry about her. Everything there was the way I'd left it, including the .38 which I kept on the top shelf of my closet. I took it down now and put it under the mattress, just in case, although I didn't expect more trouble. If someone had wanted to kill me they would have done it out on the road. I'd call Eddie Pasos in the morning.

I turned off the lights just as the sun turned the ridgeline red. I lay in the dark breathing the smell of bougainvillea that came from the garden and trying to picture who it had been.

Chapter

—7—

I was on a beach, some palm trees standing behind me. I was digging in the sand with both hands, trying to find somebody who was buried there. I scooped out sand and for a moment I saw a face, a woman's face. Not enough to recognize her or enough to know if she were alive or dead. And then the sand caved in and covered her again and I started scooping desperately. But I couldn't see her and I scooped some more. Then behind me a bird squawked. I thought it was in the palm tree, but there was no bird. It squawked again and I woke from the dream and sat up. It was Ollie squawking in the garden. And then I heard Jacoba. She was squawking too, arguing with somebody at the door. I got up, slipped on some clothes and went out.

I had planned to call Eddie Pasos first thing to tell

him about my little incident of the night before, but it turned out I didn't have to. Eddie had come to see me. At the time I didn't make anything of it.

I found Jacoba at the door talking to him and two other characters who looked like plainclothes cops. I told Jacoba to let them in. Eddie, dressed in royal blue shirt and white slacks, came and shook my hand.

"*Buenos días*, Jack. I'm sorry to bother you this early."

Then he held up a bronze-colored shell casing like the one I'd picked up the night before.

"Some of your neighbors down the hill say they heard shooting last night from this direction and we have found these next to the road. They are from an assault rifle, which in Costa Rica is an illegal weapon."

I reached into my pants pocket and pulled out a shell casing just like it.

"It looks like the same kind of stuff somebody shot at my car last night."

Eddie got a concerned look, took the casing from me, frowned at it and then at me the way cops tend to sometimes, as if I was the one who had fired the rounds and not been the target.

"Somebody tried to kill you?"

"I'm not sure. They might have been hoping I went off the road and down into the *barranca*. That way nobody would raise the question of killing—it would be an accident. But then maybe they were just trying to worry me. Anyway, I was going to call you first thing."

I told him about the shots that came out of the vegetation and then seeing the car head back down the hill. He sent his two men to scour the scene and go talk to neighbors. Jacoba brought coffee then and we went out to the patio and sat down. The rain of the night before had left the garden smelling like a jungle.

"So who is this you are talking about, Jack? Who would do this?"

I shrugged.

"I had a bit of trouble at The Tropical last night. Pepe Esparza and some of his friends wanted to turn the place into a kind of political boxing ring. I had to throw one of them out."

"And you think they wanted to give you trouble for that?" He sounded like he didn't believe it.

I sipped my coffee.

"Who knows? I've had lots of people taking an unhealthy interest in me lately. Everybody wants to talk to me and everybody wants to read my mind. Ever since Topo Morales got hit. Also, people are telling me all sorts of things I don't know much about and don't understand."

Eddie's little moustache wriggled then.

"What kind of things?"

"Like the fact that there are Colombian drug people who have been in town and also a guy named Cassanova, Raul Cassanova, who I've never heard of. Have you?"

Eddie shook his head.

"No, I haven't."

"Well. Maybe you better run his name through your computer down at headquarters. He's here on a visit."

Eddie took out a pen and jotted it down. I asked him, "Any progress in finding who killed Topo?"

He shook his head.

"We don't know yet. It's difficult because there are so many people who had reason to kill him."

"Yes. I'd say motives are the least of your problem with Topo."

Eddie fingered his moustache.

"There is one thing," he said. He looked at me, as if deciding whether to tell me. I tried to look trustworthy. "We checked the telephone records for the hotel where Morales stayed under an alias after he arrived here from Nicaragua," he said. "There was one number in Managua that was called three times in one day. We checked it out in Nicaragua, which was difficult because some government numbers up there are almost impossible to get, but we were able through our embassy to find out where he called. The number belonged to an office in the organ of Nicaraguan state security. In fact, it is the number of the top officer in charge of internal security. His name is Victor Mena."

Ollie squawked and Eddie stroked his stash a bit more, making a show of looking out into the garden.

"You know this Mena, don't you?" he said. "And so did Morales, from the days of the insurrection."

My coffee cup was halfway to my mouth and stayed there a few moments.

"You shouldn't try and be cute, Eddie. It isn't your style."

El comisionado fixed on me now.

"They say Mena still has his people here, Jack."

"I haven't seen or talked to Mena since nineteen seventy-nine," I said flatly. "Whether Topo did or not I don't know. That's the whole story."

Eddie watched me a few moments as if he'd spiked the coffee with truth serum and my skin would change color if I lied.

"If you say that, Jack, I believe it." He wasn't entirely convinced, I could tell. But I guess he could see

96

it would do no good to press me. He sipped his coffee and took his time.

"I understand Isla put on quite a show last night," he said after a while. "Despite the problems this week, I hear The Tropical was full."

"More or less."

He smiled pleasantly, but he had other business in his eyes.

"You have made your club into a very interesting, very attractive place, Jack, and it attracts certain people."

"It attracts *all* kinds of people," I said.

Eddie nodded in agreement, not looking at me.

"You don't know them all, but everybody knows you," he said. "Many of these people have business between them." He put a little spin on the word business.

"And it's their business and not mine," I said.

"Yes, I know. But then people do tell you things, Jack. They know that you are acquainted with everyone. You have connections. And they consider you *simpático*." He looked at me now over the rim of his coffee cup.

"They may ask you to pass on certain information—" he arched his eyebrows then—"or maybe not to pass it on."

I started to protest, but Eddie held up a hand.

"All I'm saying, Jack, is to remember what I told you before," he said, speaking deliberately. "That you should take into account your interests, but also our interests in this country. They are, to a great degree, the same. That is what we all want, to survive these times. If it pleases God."

I toasted Eddie with my coffee.

"I'm with you."

Eddie drank up then and I saw him out.

After he was gone I went back out to the patio, sat and thought it out, staring at the thick vegetation on the mountainside and listening to Ollie's chatter. After a while I picked up the phone and tried to call the Dessert Man at the Hotel Guerrero where he lived. I didn't like people taking potshots at me, even if their aim wasn't any good, and I wanted him to know about it. I was told he wasn't around.

Then I dug out the card Lucia Lara from the Nicaraguan embassy had given me. I wanted to talk to her about phone calls to Victor Mena and about lies. I called the number there and was told the embassy was closed on Saturday, and that, anyway, Ms. Lara had left for Managua that morning and would not be back until Monday or Tuesday.

I hung up and stared out over San José. I didn't like this information about the phone calls to Managua and Eddie's little warnings about surviving. I could see myself getting caught in the works or getting chewed up by them.

I thought about it a while more and then I found Renard's number. He had been in Nicaragua lately. So had Topo and so was Victor Mena.

He answered the phone after about eight rings and sounded groggy.

"A long night last night, Jacques," he said. "An English girl here on vacation. Another international incident."

I said I needed to talk to him and we agreed to meet for lunch in the Cafe Mundo.

Renard sipped his Bloody Mary with a slightly shaky hand. We were sitting back away from the sidewalk so the bright noonday sun wouldn't hit us even on the rebound. The ceiling fans sliced the thick, humid air. The park across the street was full of families, vendors selling ice cream et cetera. Renard squinted at them.

"Domesticity is a wonderful thing, Jacques. The English girl and I were talking about it last night at my place. English girls are not quite Nicaraguan girls, but it is not true the derogatory things that are said about them."

"I'd rather talk to you about Nicaragua," I said. "I'll give you a scoop if you'll sit on it a few days."

He brightened up. So I told him what Eddie Pasos had given me about the phone calls to Mena. Renard whistled.

"This is quite something, Jacques. And it is very good of you to tell me it." He was staring off into the plaza as if he were seeing the headlines of his story and the commotion it would cause.

"Did you ever bump into Topo when he was up in Managua?" I asked.

He shook me off.

"No, I haven't seen him up there since the first year after the insurrection. I didn't know he went there anymore. And of course I would have told you if I had."

"How about Mena? When was the last time you saw him?"

"It has been years." He got a knowing look on his face. "Major Mena is not seen often in public and he does not give interviews to journalists. Given his job in security, what he knows he chooses to keep to himself and not advertise it in newspapers for the world to know. But you are always hearing rumors about him. He is like a phantom. He seems to know everything and be everywhere. Of course this is the kind of image the chief of internal security tries to create. It makes his enemies worry about him."

I thought about that.

"I'm sorry I can't help you more with this, Jacques," Renard said.

I sipped my coffee and watched the families lining up for the buses in front of the park.

I asked Renard: "How about a guy named Raul Cassanova? Ever heard of him?"

The Frenchman's eyes lit up now.

"Oh yes, Jacques. That is one I know about. I have been tracking him for years." He leaned towards me. "And I know he is here now. Cassanova the Cuban."

"He's Cuban, not Colombian?"

"Oh yes. Extremely Cuban," he said. "But he is friends with the Colombians."

Renard's eyes filled with mischief and he pulled his chair close to the table as if he was about to eat. Gossip was his meat.

"Raul Cassanova was born in Cuba," he said. "At the time that Castro came out of the Sierra Maestra and made his move to take power, Cassanova was a young cadet in the army training school. The army took the cadets, put rifles in their hands and sent them out to defend the capital. They fought harder than a lot of the officers who were already jumping on planes and trying to get away. The swine!"

"I'd say."

"In the end, of course, Havana fell, and Cassanova's family managed to get him out on a boat and headed for Miami. That was the first time he fought against Castro, when he was only a boy. That experience it has shaped his life."

He sipped his drink.

"So he ended up in Miami," I said.

"That's right, and the next year the anti-Castro Cubans started to form the Two-five-oh-six Brigade that would make the invasion of Cuba, and Cassanova he was one of the first to sign up."

"That was the Bay of Pigs fiasco," I said.

"That's right. Cassanova was sent to Guatemala where the CIA set up training camps for the invasion force and then later he was sent to the Caribbean coast of Nicaragua where the boats would be launched. Somoza's brother saw them off personally. Cassanova, who was the youngest of the soldiers, was very impressed by that."

"Yeah, the Somozas were very impressive," I said, sipping my coffee.

Renard shook his head ruefully.

"Of course, the Bay of Pigs was a disaster. The invasion force was destroyed in three days. It was very bad for everyone, but especially for Cassanova the boy because he was captured with the rest of his unit on the first day. He spent the next eighteen months in jail, rotten Cuban jails, until the U.S. government paid the ransom of medicines to Castro to get them out. They sent Cassanova and the others back to Miami where of course the CIA was waiting for them with open arms and explanations."

"That's quite a life already."

Renard nodded enthusiastically.

"He is maybe twenty-one by this time, Jacques. The age that many boys start a career, and Cassanova does too. He goes to work for the CIA and it is only the beginning. His career is to fight Castro. They train him first and then he begins work. Driving fast boats at night, landing on the coast, planting a bomb, blowing up a boat in a harbor, poisoning a well, shooting a guard. By the time he was twenty-one years old, Cassanova could kill you in a variety of ways. When the Mafia agrees to try to assassinate Castro it is said that Cassanova is in on the planning."

Renard leaned forward again and tapped my knee. "This is important because it is the first time he has contact with the people who sell drugs."

"He has a taste for narcotics, does he?"

Renard sucked on a cigarette and blew out a plume of smoke and shook his head.

"Not a taste, but a way of always being around them no matter where he is in the world. This is the late sixties now, the CIA it has not been able to kill Castro and the U.S. government is tired of wasting money so that Cassanova can blow up rowboats on the coast of Cuba. The CIA has more important problems now anyway: in Southeast Asia. By now, Cassanova he is married to the daughter of an American military officer, he speaks English, his neighbors think he works for an import-export business, which is really one of the shadow companies of the CIA. Cassanova tells his neighbors that the company is transferring him to Bangkok in Thailand. Where he really goes is to Laos to train hill people, to work in the secret war there. Again he gets mixed up with the drug business."

"The Golden Triangle," I said.

"Yes. This time it is the heroin smugglers in Laos. The Laotians will work with the CIA against the Vietnamese, but only if they are allowed to continue their heroin smuggling. No one has ever been able to stop the smuggling anyway, so the CIA goes along."

Renard smoked and gave me his clever, mischievous look. "This is quite something, isn't it, Jacques?" he said.

"How do you know all this about Cassanova?" I ask him.

He just wriggled his eyebrows.

"Cassanova is a man people don't forget, Jacques. He is flamboyant. People remember him and some people don't like him. A reporter's work is easier if your subject has enemies."

"Then what?"

He sipped his Bloody Mary.

"After the fall of Saigon, Cassanova is sent back to Miami and life becomes difficult. It is the years the CIA is being investigated, many operations are canceled. Cassanova and other Cubans who had worked ever since nineteen sixty for the CIA they are out of work, with no money coming in and Castro still in Cuba. Cassanova and others, they get angry. And that is when they find new employers who are looking for men with their specific talents: Colombia's drug smugglers, the biggest cocaine-smuggling operation in the world."

I thought of what Frankie Quintero had told me about recent visitors to our fair city, but I didn't want to interrupt him.

"So he's back with the drug boys," I said.

Renard smoked and nodded.

"They fly the cocaine into the Bahamas, put it on the fast boats to the coast of Florida. People like Cassanova, using their CIA training, are the perfect operators. They know fast boats, communications, the coast of Florida—and weapons, just in case they have to fight the Coast Guard or the Drug Enforcement agents."

Renard smiled and lifted his eyebrows.

"Isn't that just perfect."

"Lovely," I agreed.

"In the early eighties, when the CIA begins to form the Contra army to fight the Sandinista communists, Cassanova has money in the bank and is ready again to join the 'good fight' as you call it. He trains Contras in Honduras and he goes into combat with them, even though he is now forty years old." Renard shrugged. "Then, of course, your American Congress gets angry with the Contras for killing too many civilians, putting bombs in ports, and it cuts off the money. People in your own government begin selling arms to the Iranians secretly to support the war and it all comes apart."

Renard exhaled, and looked at it as if he was watching the whole scheme go up in smoke. Then he looked at me.

"Then a month ago, or so, Cassanova showed up here in Costa Rica."

"What do you think he's up to here?" I asked.

Renard cocked his head in thought.

"People say Costa Rica is now the perfect place to transship drugs, Jacques, or at least to refuel planes. There is no army, no radar, no air force planes, and many small landing strips on private farms. You also have a population that does not like the Sandinistas and would not mind funding the war against them."

"So you think Cassanova is here doing drug business, but maybe in order to funnel money to the Contras."

Renard shrugged.

"I don't know. Maybe he is just here on vacation, but I am looking around."

"Is that what you were doing up at the northern border?"

Renard squinted at me cleverly, but didn't answer. I told him then what Frankie had told me about the

Colombians without mentioning Frankie. He let that information lie on the table between us and examined it a bit.

"And who are these Colombians, Jacques?"

"I don't know that. I make it a point not to know Colombians."

"And I'm sure you don't want to tell me who told you."

I shook my head and he smiled.

"That's all right, Jacques. It is still helpful. I have other sources."

"The question is what does all this have to do with Topo getting hit? I can't see Topo mixed up with guys this big."

Renard shrugged.

"There are small fish in every organization, Jacques. In time, they get eaten up by the larger fish. Topo he was eaten."

I nodded.

"Yes, and I don't want the same sharks to come for me," I said.

"Don't worry, Jacques. I will go to my sources. We will see what is happening here and do it quickly so you can feel safer and I can get back to Europe to keep my very important appointment." He meant with his daughter. "But right now I have another appointment with the English lady."

I told Renard I'd grab the check and I watched him walk across the plaza and turn the corner out of sight.

Chapter

—8—

To days later, things got even hotter down in our tropical paradise.

First thing in the morning, I opened the newspaper and on the page where they printed crime news I found a long article all about the Medellín Cartel. Maybe it was just a coincidence, but then again maybe it wasn't. Somebody might have been sending a message to the new arrivals in the city, the cocaine boys.

The headline said: "Twenty Years of Crime: Drug Mafia Threatens Caribbean." It didn't say who had written the story, if it was an agency wire or a local reporter. Given the record of the Medellín Cartel, a reporter wouldn't want his name on it. He could end up dead.

The article was a history of the drug-smuggling organization. How the families started in the late sixties and early seventies moving cocaine from South America to the United States, building a whole new criminal network along the way. The article told how they got peasants to grow the stuff secretly in Peru and Bolivia. Then they processed it at clandestine laboratories in Colombia, loaded it onto small planes flown by pilots of various nationalities, including Americans. Sometimes they offloaded it to fast boats in the Bahamas, driven by pilots, people like Cassanova, who ferried it to Florida. The coke was delivered to middlemen, usually Miami Cubans, who cut it and put it on the street.

Then the article talked about the early eighties in Miami when the Cubans and the Colombians fought a battle for control of the industry. For a couple of years, these guys were gunning for each other in bars, restaurants, from passing cars. Sometimes they used assault rifles, firing them on automatic, emptying full clips right in downtown Miami. It was like Chicago in the twenties. The police figured that in a couple of years two hundred fifty of these Latin gangsters ended up dead. The local business leaders tore out their hair, saying the tourist trade was being ruined by the war on the streets. Nobody wanted to spend two weeks vacationing in Miami worrying about catching a stray bullet.

Finally it quieted down, and the cocaine bosses in Colombia began to work together. They held a first meeting, something like the U.S. Mafia's summit back in the nineteen fifties at Appalachin. And just like the Mafia they began to move out of the shadows and branch out into legitimate enterprise. They bought pieces of banks, newspapers, real estate in Colombia and Miami. They went into politics by buying Colombian politicians. In time, they had even cut a deal with a leftist guerrilla group to act as security guards for their laboratories in the jungle. When the minister of justice became too much of a bother, the Medellín boys had him gunned down.

Now, there was pressure on them in the Bahamas and other islands of the Caribbean from the U.S. drug people, but they were still making money hand over fist. That's where the article ended.

What it didn't say was that maybe they had come to Costa Rica. Like Renard said, it was the ideal place: no army, no air force, no radar. With war already threatening the country from the north, these visitors from the south were all we needed. I read the article over and wondered again who had put it in the newspaper. Somebody was pulling strings behind the scenes and I wondered who it was.

After a while, I got up, got ready and drove down to the club. The place was closed on Monday and that was the day I used to take care of business. First, I had to barter with a liquor salesman who was peddling cut-rate scotch, supposedly hijacked off a ship in the Panama Canal. I paid him off. Then there was a health inspector who got a couple of free drinks and a pass to Friday night's show with Isla.

I was just seeing him out when this tall police lieutenant came in the door asking for me. He said Eddie Pasos wanted to see me right away and that he would take me to him. I asked him what it was about, but all he'd say is that it was urgent.

So I locked the place again and got in the government car. The driver turned on his siren, did a lot of fancy speeding, but didn't say a word. We sped through the middle of town, past the cathedral and the central park, and then went south on Calle Cinco—Fifth Street.

It took us into what served as the red light district of San José, a grid of narrow streets, flyblown bars and tinderbox hotels with hourly rates. The roar of old rattletrap buses filled the streets, that and the humid afternoon heat, which seemed like it had melted the sagging electrical wires. The old clapboard bars weren't exactly competition for The Tropical. They had names like the Montecarlo, Pigalle, The Golden Falcon. They were painted bright colors and jukeboxes blasting from inside each one day and night. Usually some singer pleading in Spanish for a lost love, like the machines were calling to each other. They shared the streets with produce stands so that the neighborhood smelled of decaying fruit. Between the bars and the food stands were the second-floor walk-up hotels so that the girls didn't have to drag their customers too far.

The girls who hung out in the bars were also overripe and pleading for love. The lips were all painted blood red. Sometimes they stood in the doorways. They puckered as you drove past and the eyes lit up with phony delight. The government car got stopped in traffic and a dark brown woman in a flowered dress with a big red poinsettia in her hair shot me a fiery look and then laughed out loud, showing me all her bad teeth.

The police car stopped in front of a run-down hotel called La Costa del Sol, the Sunny Coast. But this place wasn't sunny at all, especially now with another three cop cars outside it. Eddie was standing on the sidewalk.

"Sorry to disturb you again, Jack, but it is necessary."

He led me into a dark, soiled lobby. In a room beyond it someone was cooking, it smelled like a com-

bination of rancid meat and coconut. The old propri-
etress held a big key ring and was rattling on about
how she didn't know who the man was. She was a
fat, light-skinned woman with rouged cheeks, wearing a torn flowered housedress, the kind of woman
who would always look as if she had just dragged herself out of bed.

She led us slowly up the splintered red stairs—red
stairs, I guess, got you in the mood for sex—and then
down a very narrow corridor to the last door on the
left. Eddie pushed it open. The room was a faded pink
color with washed-out red curtains pulled open. A
beam of dusty light fell through the window. On the
bed there was a bloodstained sheet with flies on it and
under it you could see a body.

Eddie walked over, pulled the sheet back, and the
flies scattered. It was Chelly, the pilot. He had lost a
lot of blood and looked paler than before. His blue
eyes were wide open so that he looked even more
spaced out than usual. That was the way it should be,
I guess, he was staring at eternity.

Eddie held the sheet back a few moments to give
me a good look. There was a deep gash in the neck,
right around the jugular, which is where all the blood
had escaped.

"Have you seen him before?"

"Yes, I know him," I said. "Or I did. They called
him Chelly. He was an American and he flew small
planes."

Eddie nodded and stayed looking at the corpse as if
he expected Chelly to verify the information.

"It appears he was killed with a knife," Eddie said.

"And not a very clean job of it," I said. "Probably
a whore who wanted all his money. A guy like Chelly,
he'd seem like a millionaire to one of these girls."

Eddie was shaking his head.

"The woman who runs the place said he came in last night with a woman, a prostitute, but she says she can't remember which one. Still, the motive was not robbery. He had a little money in his pockets, and he has a ring and a bracelet, both gold." He lifted the sheet so I could see them on Chelly's pale hand and wrist. "A whore and an accomplice, probably her pimp, who killed him in order to rob him would not leave those things. They would take them from the corpse."

"Maybe they got scared off."

Eddie shook his head.

"No. Apparently no one heard anything," he said. "It rained last night and the sound against this tin roof would cover the sound of the crime." He shrugged. "But then the people in a place such as this, they might not tell you anyway, even if they heard him being murdered."

He dropped the sheet back over Chelly's face. He looked around with an expression of distaste on his face. Eddie had been a cop a long time and had been in scenes like this one before. But he had never allowed it to rub off on him. He was still the gentleman cop. Right now, in his spit-and-polish uniform, he looked like he had just parachuted into the place by mistake.

We were standing there when another uniformed officer came into the room. I recognized him. He was a major in the Narcotics Section of the Department of Justice and his name was Mejia. He'd been in the club a few times. He was a large, dark man with the face and body of a bull and muddy brown eyes. Eddie went to him, they conferred, then he picked up the sheet, looked at Chelly without a trace of emotion, dropped the sheet, nodded at Eddie and then went out of the room to talk to more uniformed men.

Eddie turned to me:

"You say he flies planes. Who was it he worked for?"

"Over the years, just about anybody." I told him the story of Chelly flying in Vietnam and then his freelancing. "Lately they say he was doing some work for the Contras."

Eddie nodded.

"Flying arms and munitions."

"The last time he talked to me, a few days ago, he said he was flying air."

Eddie frowned.

"And that, what does it mean?"

I shrugged.

"You got me. But that's what he said. He was flying planeloads of air and somebody was paying him to do it."

"When was it, the last time you saw him?"

"Maybe three days ago. It was Friday. The floor show was on."

Eddie was looking at me suspiciously, as if this business about the air was some kind of gringo joke between me and the dead man.

"Have you ever heard that he transported drugs?"

"I never heard that specifically, but that doesn't mean he didn't," I said. "I think he had a taste for the stuff."

"Did he have any friends, close associates?"

I thought about it.

"Not really. He came into the club sometimes, but always by himself."

Eddie nodded and reached into his pocket. He brought out a red gambling chip. It was one from my club. It said "The Tropical" on it.

"We found this in his pocket," he said.

I took it from him.

"Must have been an unlucky chip," I said. I was thinking of how Chelly had always talked about being lucky and how his luck had finally run out.

Eddie was watching me carefully.

"Did you ever see him in the company of anyone from the diplomatic corps? With a foreign diplomat stationed here in San José?"

It was my turn to frown at him. It was a strange question, but I could see Eddie had reasons for asking it.

"Chelly wasn't in that class," I told him. "He didn't hang out with embassy people. Why do you ask?"

He reached into his pocket and pulled out a calling card.

"Because we found this also in his shirt pocket along with the chip. I thought he might have come across them both at the same place, at your club."

He handed it to me. I'd seen one just like it, not too long before. It said Lucia Lara, Embassy of the Republic of Nicaragua.

I guess I looked surprised. Eddie was watching me with interest.

"Do you know her?"

"A bit. She's been to the club and she also came to see me a few days ago to ask about Topo. Just like everybody else in town."

The wheels were turning behind Eddie's eyes.

"You didn't know her before?"

I had to smile; it was Eddie following his guerrilla conspiracy theory.

"No, I didn't," I said.

He took the card back from me.

"I thought you might have known her years ago during the insurrection," he said. "You knew Victor Mena and she was his lover."

My eyebrows went up. I had asked her if she knew Victor and she had said only that she had heard of him. She was a good liar.

"It must have been before my time," I said to Eddie. "I didn't meet her until a few days ago. But you know how it is in San José, sooner or later, everybody knows everybody else."

I said it as a throwaway line. I didn't realize right then just how true that was.

Chapter
—9—

I had Eddie's uniformed driver drop me downtown on Primera Avenida. It was lunch hour, cars were battling it out in the streets and people were marching at me down the sidewalks. I ducked into a dive I knew down there to have a drink and get out of harm's way.

I ordered a drink and observed a few minutes of silence in memory of Chelly. We hadn't been big buddies, Chelly and I, but he always paid his tab and he was an American. It wasn't every day that an American in Central America got blown away. Given recent events—Topo getting killed and then the shots at me in the middle of the night—I didn't like the connotation. Like I said, I felt all of a sudden I was caught in the middle of some business I didn't understand and these days in Central America the middle was a dangerous place to be.

I thought about it a bit more and the longer I did,

the more irritated I got. After a couple of *mojitos* I decided what to do and I hit the street.

I walked the three blocks to the Hotel Guerrero where the Dessert Man had established his headquarters. The middle-level Contra boys who were allowed in the country were garrisoned there. There were usually a few American men registered as well who listed themselves as tourists or maybe consultants. Everybody knew they were CIA types and what they were consulting about was the war. The management didn't have to worry about the tourist season ending. In Central America these days war was always in season.

From the outside, the Guerrero was a big old Spanish colonial fortress. Inside it was neo-Miami. The lobby was plated floor to ceiling with mirrors, so that nobody could get the drop on you, and lots of potted palms grew in the corners where the bodyguards loitered, making sure the wrong people didn't try to check in.

There was usually one of those guards standing duty, but now there were at least three, one posted at the entrance—he was the doorman—and a couple of "bellboys" in the lobby.

I walked in, watching twenty versions of myself, the guards and the palm trees reproduced in the lobby mirrors. We looked like a convention. I walked to the in-house phones, called the Dessert Man's suite and he said he would send somebody down for me.

I bought a three-day-old American newspaper at the newsstand and sat down on a red plush sofa, while the guards watched me. I looked at the headlines, about an assassination in Northern Ireland, rioting in South Africa, a city bombed in Afghanistan. Then I read an article about the death of Topo. The reporter referred to "a culture of violence in Central America" that had not before infected Costa Rica. Some culture.

I was sitting there when the elevator doors opened, a small dark guy stuck his head out, reconnoitered the lobby a moment and then motioned to me. I got in and he took me up. He was a young man with a face pitted by acne, as if he'd gotten hit with buckshot. He was wearing a long white shirt and dark pants, like anybody might wear, but he also had on canvas-and-rubber jungle boots, the kind you wore if you hiked a lot through tropical mountains. The shirt covered his waist but you could see the bulge there where he had his pistol hidden. He was quite an elevator operator.

We went right to the top and the doors opened. The Elevator Boy marched me down the red-carpeted hall under gaudy chandeliers. We passed some closed doors. One of them opened and a man came out dressed in camouflage pants. He glanced at me and then disappeared into a door across the hall.

We marched all the way to the end of the corridor where the Elevator Boy knocked on the door of Suite 800. Outside the door was a restaurant cart with a dozen empty plates on it; probably what was left of the Dessert Man's midafternoon snack. We went in and the Elevator Boy got me to sit on another red plush sofa under a phony chandelier and then he disappeared through a door that led to one of the bedrooms.

The room I was in held the high ground in San José; there were windows overlooking the street and most of the rooftops of the city. You could see all the way out to where I lived, the hills on the outskirts.

One of the walls of the room was covered with a large military operational map. I got up for a closer look and recognized detailed parts of the northern mountains and southern cattle country of Nicaragua, the main combat zones where the war was being fought. The map was studded with red and white pins which marked the opposing forces.

Next to the map was a closet, open a crack. As I started to turn away I noticed a rifle leaning there. I looked at it closely. It was an AK-47, an attack rifle used a lot by the Contras which used the same kind of ammunition I'd found next to the road after I was shot at. Hanging above it was a set of camouflage fatigues. I could see the Dessert Man sitting up there at night dressed in his uniform, with his rifle, his color television and the portable bar he had set up, sitting under the chandelier, moving pins, making believe he was a general.

I was standing there when a bedroom door opened and a couple of Contras walked out. They were dressed like the Elevator Boy, in civvies, but they wore the same telltale boots. One of them I recognized, he was a rebel commander and his nom de guerre was Paraiso—Paradise. Dark, with long hair and a thick, tangled beard, he was probably no more than thirty, but his face was lined by the sun, and looked older. His eyes were jet black and he moved skittishly, as if he could sense that he was way out of place in the hotel. He was like some exotic animal captured by one of the guests.

I recognized him because he had been in The Tropical one time with the Dessert Man when he was out of Nicaragua for rest and relaxation. And I remembered now that he had been one of the Nicaraguans drinking in the club the night Topo died. His eyes fell on me as he walked past, and he squinted at me. I looked familiar, some breed of creature spotted somewhere before, but he wasn't sure where. He didn't say anything. He shot me a last look as he was moving out the door and then he was gone.

I was still looking over that way when the Dessert Man squeezed his way through the doorframe of the bedroom and waddled towards me. He wasn't wearing his usual wall-to-wall smile. What he did have on was a green silk shirt with a pink flamingo on it. He steered towards me with his hand out ready to shake, like the rudder on a blimp.

"Hello, Jack," he said. "You heard about the pilot. They shoot him down."

I didn't take the hand.

"Yes, I heard. Probably the same soldiers who opened up on me the other day at five o'clock in the morning," I said, pointing at the rifle in the closet. "Except they hit Chelly because they had him point blank."

He frowned at me. When the Dessert Man frowned his face looked like a bowl of whipping cream with waves in it.

"Jack, I swear to God at five o'clock I was sleeping right here in my bunk." Except he pronounced it boonk. "I already tell Captain Pasos. I have nothing to do with this." He bunched his fat fingers into a fist and kissed the thumb. "I swear it."

"But a couple of your buddies did," I told him, getting up in his face, or as close as I could given his forty-eight-inch stomach. I was thinking now of the two soldiers who had just sidled out. "They were taking target practice with their AK-forty-sevens. I know it was your boys because they missed as usual. But I still don't like it. The next time I shoot back and I yell bloody murder until they drive you out of this town."

I jabbed my finger into his fat chest and it sank in a ways. My stomach hit his and I felt metal under the pink flamingo. I picked up the edge of the shirt and there was the pistol imbedded in the fat, like it had melted into a can of lard. He pulled his shirt down and shook his head.

"I am sorry for the incident at your club the other night," he said. "But we have nothing to do with this aggression against you, Jack, or any other shooting. We are armed only to protect ourselves."

I just watched him breathe now, the flamingo going up and down on his chest. The Elevator Boy had come out as well and he was watching me and looking nervous, his hand playing near his hip. The Dessert Man took me by the arm then and led me across the room back to the sofa.

"Let's have a drink, Jack, and we can talk about this trouble."

He waddled to a bar near the window, brought me a rum and tonic and poured himself a banana daiquiri out of a pitcher he kept. He sat down across from me in a red satin chair that exhaled under his weight. The map hung just behind him and the Dessert Man sat in his flamingo shirt sipping his daiquiri and started talking as if he were the commander in chief deciding the future of the conflict.

"The war it is finally coming here, Jack. Our enemies they sense we will not be defeated and they are expanding the theater of the war. Human life here it is now being made very cheap."

I squinted at him.

"Some people are making it cheap," I said.

"It is not us," the Dessert Man said. "We have no reason to kill people here. Our insurgency it is in Nicaragua. But if they come after us here, we will protect ourselves. And we have intelligence that they will. Just as they have gone after Topo and the pilot."

I shot him my best skeptical glance.

"Why would the Sandinistas kill Chelly after all these years?"

"Because he fly arms, ammunition and medical supplies for us, Jack," he said. "Everybody they know that. And because during the insurrection he fly arms for them. Chelly he was a mercenary, he fly for whoever they pay him. But to the Sandinistas maybe they consider he is traitor to them. Just like they know Topo was a traitor to them."

What he said was true; Chelly had flown supply missions into northern Costa Rica near the end of the fight in '79, years ago. Of course, he had done it for a price, but still he'd done it.

The Dessert Man sipped his daiquiri and looked into my eyes now.

"Maybe they will think you are also a traitor to them because you are here in Costa Rica. Just like the other two. You must be very careful, Jack. Anything can happen here."

He let that sink in. I sipped my drink and said nothing. He lifted his bulk out of the chair, went to the bar, poured himself more banana drink and stood near the window blocking most of the light.

"It was just a matter of time, Jack, before the violence it comes here," he said. "This place it has lived many years at peace, while everyone else they are fighting. But this is the way it began in Nicaragua, Salvador, Guatemala. One person dead, then another. In no time, you have a guerrilla war."

I gazed around the plush hotel suite.

"And here you are in the thick of the battle," I said.

He turned towards me.

"Today we have more reports of combat up near the border," he said. "Also in the last few days we have received intelligence of flights that are unexplained over northern Costa Rica. Maybe they are reconnaissance flights. Maybe the Sandinistas they are planning something. We don't know. We have told our troops to come south, closer to the border. It is very serious. All of Central America it could blow up, Jack."

He walked back, sat down in the red chair and tapped me on the knee.

"If I am you, Jack, I get out now. I sell The Tropical and I take my money and I runs."

I looked at Pepe long and hard.

"That's just great," I said. "First you pick a fight with me at the club. Then somebody shoots at me and now you try to tell me the war is coming and I should sell the club. I must say that's pretty subtle business maneuvering. I suppose you're ready to make me an offer."

I sipped my rum. I wondered if that was the scam: to make people scared that the enemy was on his way and then buy them out cheap. Pepe looked hurt.

"I tell you, Jack, the war it is coming. There will be fighting here and all over the region. These killings are only the first."

"I don't buy it," I told him. "And the cops don't either. As a matter of fact I know what they're thinking. They're figuring Chelly got hit because of drugs."

The fat man's face wrinkled again and behind his eyes a thought crossed from one side to another and tried to hide. There had always been insinuations that the Contras had ties to drug operators who helped them transship arms, but there had never been hard proof. The Dessert Man didn't like this little foray of mine, but I went after him.

"Maybe Chelly was moving both arms and drugs as

part of the resupply operations," I said. "Is that it? And maybe he ripped off some coke or scammed some of the guns."

The Dessert Man was swiveling his head back and forth like an antiaircraft gun trying to shoot my words out of the sky.

"We know nothing of drugs."

"Who was it who got to Chelly, the military boys or one of the drug connections?"

"We have no drug connections."

"Oh, no? How about Mr. Cassanova."

It was a shot in the dark, but the moment I said it I knew I'd hit the target. The Dessert Man's mouth opened in an O like it had hit him right in the gut.

"I'm told the Cuban gentleman is in town," I said. "I've never met him, but I understand he has a long record in clandestine operations."

Pepe's mouth closed and he watched me now as if I was walking near a land mine or doing something equally stupid and dangerous.

"You should be careful, Jack. You don't want to talk about people and things you don't know." He said this in his best edgy understatement, something he'd picked up from American gangster movies. "He is a man of long and violent experience and he has friends, as you say, in high places."

I stirred my rum.

"You mean the Medellín boys," I said. "Very high, indeed. Are they your 'beezness' associates too?"

Pepe became grave then.

"Cassanova has a long history of serving the interests of your government and he has friends there too."

"Oh, yes? Like who?"

"Like Colonel Akers in your own embassy." Pepe said it as if that would shut me up.

125

I frowned.

"Colonel Akers? He introduced himself to me as Mr. Akers. That's quite a promotion."

Pepe had his lips pressed closed now so that nothing else would escape that shouldn't get out.

"I didn't tell you anything," he said. "But you don't want to get mixed up in this, Jack. I'm telling you for your own good."

Hearing him reminded me of what Topo had said the night he died; there were people in town and important things were happening.

I drained the drink, got up, and so did he. I sank a finger into the Dessert Man's chest again.

"As long as nobody takes any more potshots at me and doesn't disrupt my club, I don't care what they do."

"That's fine, Jack."

Just then there was a sharp rap on the door behind me, like a gunshot. I turned and the door opened. It was Paradise and his friend, making believe they were room service. They glanced at me again with their dead eyes and went into the bedroom.

"And keep those guerrilla kids away from me and my club."

Pepe's head nodded on its fleshy springs.

"Okay, Jack."

The Elevator Boy took me back down then, passing the platoon of guards down in the lobby. I waved goodbye to them where they were hiding behind the potted palms.

Then I walked back to the club wondering just what the connection was between Cassanova the Cuban and "Colonel" Akers of the U.S. embassy and wondering, too, if I didn't already know too much.

Chapter

—10—

I let myself into the club, grabbed a bottle of rum and took a ringside seat at the edge of the empty dance floor. The place was dark and quiet and I could think about what to do.

I didn't like the Dessert Man's analysis of the situation: anything could happen, even a full-scale war. Of course, for years it had been that way in Central America. Nine years before it was unexpected events— the insurrection—that had kept me around, and it would probably be the same kind of event that drove me out. So what he said was true enough.

I always carried that idea in the back of my mind. You live in a place that isn't your own country, and you have that feeling. That it won't last forever. You're like a piece from the wrong puzzle and some day you're going to get weeded out. Especially a place like Central America which at all times is on the edge of catastrophe.

What was I still doing there if the place was a powder keg? I always told people I was there because business was good and Costa Rica was comfortable and there was no war here. It was true I lived a nice life, the club was profitable, the clientele was interesting enough and I never got tired of palm trees. But deep down that wasn't it.

Renard had said to me once:

"You're like me, Jacques. You try to tell the world you are a pragmatic businessman and a cynic. What you really are is a romantic. Me, I could be much more comfortable and make more money in Paris, but I prefer the exotic. You could make more money in New York, but you are here. Because of the place, maybe because of what happened to you here."

It was years ago he'd told me that. He was talking about her and how she was killed in '79. I told him he was crazy. What I lived with her during those last months was one thing and life running The Tropical was completely different. The Tropical was a den of vices, not all of them, but enough, and she had never stepped foot in a place like it.

"The perfect place to hide from her memory," he said.

I told him he was full of it. If I wanted to forget I would have gone back to New York.

"Exactly," he said.

So I admitted to myself that I hadn't wanted to go back right away. That I hadn't wanted to lose myself again in New York and forget about her. I had never looked at her body when she was killed, I had never seen her dead. Renard said it was as if I thought some day she would walk back into my life.

Of course, it was only for a time that lasted. But by then I had settled into my life in Costa Rica. When

I did go back to New York to visit, almost three years later, it was there I didn't fit. Now it was English that sounded foreign when I heard it on the street. It was the pace of New York that drove me crazy. It was a whole different frame of mind. There was no sense being there if I didn't feel I belonged.

So I stayed in Costa Rica and got used to being the *extranjero*, as they call you here, the stranger, the foreigner. The business had gotten better and better. And in time, there had been other women too; Costa Rica had been good to me that way. But down deep, Renard would say, I had her in my mind, I was still waiting for her to walk in.

I wasn't thinking that right at that moment. Right then I was sipping rum and mulling over what had happened to Topo and Chelly and the shots at me, and what the fat man had said. If he was right, Costa Rica would see the war, business would dry up and so would my so-called reasons for staying.

I was working that all out when I heard a door close. I looked up and Lucia Lara was standing there. She was wearing a white blouse and a tight black skirt. I said to her:

"How'd you get in here this time? Pick the lock?"

She stepped farther out of the shadows to the edge of the dance floor.

"I told the guard I had an appointment with you."

She came across the floor and stood next to the table. The light was dim but enough for me to appreciate that healthy, strapping body of hers, the broad shoulders and the breasts under the gauzy blouse.

"How was your trip, Miss Lara? That is your name, isn't it? You weren't lying about that too, were you?"

"That is my name. Why would I lie?"

I shrugged.

"I'm told you're a spy. I figured maybe you had a few names, a few identities you shopped around."

She gave me that narrow-eyed look, behind her tree again.

"Our enemies, I'm sure, say I am a spy, but they have their reasons for lying."

"As a matter of fact it wasn't a Contra who told me. I heard it from another diplomat. It seems everybody knows."

She took that in without expression.

"I am a Nicaraguan diplomat stationed in Costa Rica and so I am accused of being a spy. That is to be expected. People say these things not because they are true, but because it makes them sound clever and informed."

I sipped my drink and looked up at her.

"Do other diplomats also leave their calling cards in the pockets of dead men?"

She frowned at me then.

"The police have already been to question me today," she said. "They know I'm not guilty of any killing. I wasn't even in the country when this man died. I never met him, either in public or private. The only place I might have seen him was here in this club but I don't remember him. It is obvious to the police that my card was placed on the corpse in an attempt to implicate me and my government. If you are honest, you will recognize that as well."

I grinned at her.

"If I'm honest. That's a good one. How about the phone calls to Victor Mena made from Topo Morales's hotel room the day he died? I suppose they were also placed by the tooth fairy."

She frowned more deeply now, as if what I was

saying was impossible. She sat down in the chair next to me.

"I don't know what you're talking about."

"You should have asked Victor Mena when you were up in Managua. He could have told you."

"I didn't see Victor Mena," she said. "I'm not a spy and I don't work for him, no matter what you are told."

I let a smile play with the ends of my lips.

"Is that right? You told me you were acquainted with Mena, but now I understand at one time you were very closely acquainted. I hear you worked undercover with him."

I smiled at my own joke, but she only stared into my eyes again, the same way she had when she told me she was a liar.

"That was many years ago and for a short time," she said. "I have barely seen him since then."

I kept smiling. She said:

"Don't believe me, if you want, but I went to Managua to see my family. Even spies have families."

I sipped my drink and said nothing and she watched me do it. Then she said:

"I am told you knew this pilot who was killed."

"I knew him at the roulette wheel. That's all."

She was watching me closely now.

"I understand that he flew arms shipments for the Contras, that he was a mercenary."

"When he flew for the Sandinistas in seventy-nine he was a hero. Now that he flies for the Contras, he's nothing but a mercenary. You've developed an interesting moral code."

"So he did fly arms for them."

I shrugged.

"I wouldn't know. I just let him lose his money in my casino. And even if I did know, I wouldn't say. I don't spy on my customers."

She gave me an icy look from under her long lashes and then glanced away.

"That's right, you're not involved anymore."

"Precisely," I said. I lifted my glass. "I have enough to do worrying about my own cause these days and I don't get mixed up in other people's. I especially don't like anybody trying to get me involved against my will. Last time, in seventy-eight, you caught me at the right moment. I had nothing to lose. This time, I have my own interests to look out for. I'm not a guerrilla, I'm a barkeeper."

She watched me now the way she had the first time I'd met her, looking behind my eyes to find someone else inside me.

"I don't believe you," she said finally. "No one changes like that. You cared once, you fought for something that mattered to you."

"To kill time."

She shook her head hard and turned away. She spoke through her teeth.

"Don't tell me that. Don't tell me you had no illusions, no ideals." She kept shaking her head as if something had appeared before her and she was trying to make it go away. "When you say that, you are saying none of us had illusions. That is what our enemies tell the world. That all we ever wanted, deep inside us, was power and money. You don't have to agree with what we have done, but don't slander the ones who died." She looked at me now. "You don't live years in the mud, the way some did, just to make yourself rich and comfortable. There are easier ways to do that. Ways where you don't risk every day being killed."

I drank down what she said with some of the rum.

"That's fine, so I did my hitch and I don't want to get mixed up in it again."

"You are already mixed up in it," she said. "Everyone who lives in Central America is mixed up in it."

"Well, if that's the case you have a lot of other people to choose from, whatever it is you're looking for."

She squinted at me now, as if she were taking aim. Then she pulled the trigger.

"You say you are no longer involved. Why? Because you lost a girlfriend in the war?"

She watched me to see if her shot had hit home. It grazed me and I squinted back at her.

"Yes, I know about it," she said. "It was a tragedy, just as it was a tragedy for all the Nicaraguans who lost loved ones in the insurrection. Do you know how many were killed?"

"Too many," I said.

She leaned back in the chair, looked away and talked matter-of-factly, as if she was describing something she was seeing across the room.

"I lost two men in the war," she said. "In nineteen seventy-five, my husband was killed. The *guardia* raided a safe house where he was hiding and they shot him. He was older than I was, he was the one who had brought me into the Front and educated me about the world. I told myself I was a revolutionary, as he had been, and that I would go on. But the truth was that I was very young, my own identity had gotten lost in his and I hadn't prepared myself at all for the day he died. I went crazy for a time when he was killed. It was as if my own heart and soul were dying. That's how I felt then. I told myself I would never have another man."

She looked at me and then she shrugged.

"But in nineteen seventy-seven, I took another lover," she said. "It is hard when you are having to live a clandestine life, always hiding things from the people around, and finally you need someone you can tell everything to." She got a malicious glint in her eye. "And just as people say, we guerrillas are notoriously promiscuous amongst ourselves, since we can't trust anyone else. That affair lasted for a while. Then he was killed as well. For a time after that Victor Mena helped me."

She stopped and searched my eyes.

"You think I'm lying," she said.

I sipped my drink and didn't answer.

"You can ask the same people who told you I am a spy. They will probably know the story. My husband's death was on the front page of all the newspapers." She looked away again across the room. "I know what it is to find someone you love in the middle of a war. I know what it is to dream of peace and to live that with them. To dream of making love without having to worry that someone is coming to shoot you. You are not the only one to suffer the loss of a lover. And there were many Nicaraguans who lost even more. They had their fathers killed, mothers, brothers, sons. Tens of thousands of people were killed."

"It wasn't my war in the first place and it still isn't," I said.

She turned back to me.

"But it was *her* war."

I stopped with my drink near my lips. It was my turn to take aim at her.

"So you come to me and figure you can trade on that. Is that it? That takes a lot of idealism, a lot of illusions."

"I didn't mean that."

"Yes, you did."

"I didn't." She looked into my eyes. "But you are still blaming us for her death. As if it was her own people who killed her and not our enemies. As if we were guilty for her death. She would tell you that is wrong."

"She's not telling anything to anybody anymore."

She leaned towards me now, as if she was going to grab me and shake me, but she didn't. She clenched her fists on the table.

"Right now in Costa Rica it is like it was at the time of the insurrection," she said. "People here are having to make decisions, to take sides. People in the government and people outside the government. This moment is crucial."

I didn't know what she meant, but I didn't like the sound of it. I said:

"What is that supposed to mean?"

"You know many people and we may need you to help us. We need you to contact some people on the other side. It will be nothing illegal or violent."

"It will be nothing at all," I said.

"We are not asking you to do something only for us, but for yourself as well. It will be in your interest to help us."

I shook my head.

"I doubt it," I said. "I'm not helping anyone, you or your enemies. The Costa Ricans have been good to me and they don't want me mixed up with politics. And I'm not making contacts and ending up in the middle. That's probably what happened to Topo and to Chelly, trying to play both sides. Thanks but no thanks."

135

She watched me knock back more rum. I said:

"Go back and tell Victor Mena that this time I said no."

She shut her eyes, stayed there a few moments and then got up. She looked down at me, with a bit of a sneer.

"You are drowning yourself in liquor and in self-pity," she said. "You are killing yourself and maybe you will be responsible for killing other people as well."

She glared at me another few moments, then turned and walked back across the dance floor. I watched her go out the door.

I stayed there a while longer with the rum. Probably too long. That's why I didn't think of it then, the way she had talked about me acting in my own interest. Just the same words Eddie Pasos had used the night Topo was killed.

Chapter

—11—

THE next morning's papers had big headlines about Chelly being killed and on-the-spot photos of the room where he was found. Very pleasant. One paper also printed an article that supposedly gave the inside story on what had been going on in San José these last five days.

The article said that both Chelly and Topo Morales had once worked for the Sandinistas and there was speculation, as the Dessert Man had said, that they were killed because they were considered traitors. But there were other "sources" who claimed that lately both men had been involved in the drug trade. The paper didn't say who the sources were or what other information they had to back them up, but it put two and two together. It was suspected by some officials that the Sandinistas themselves were moving drugs, that there might have been a falling-out with their

henchmen and the bullets had started to fly on Costa
Rican soil. The U.S. had made the same accusation
about drugs a few years back, but then it had faded
from the news. Maybe the Sandinistas were in the
business after all. The paper said if that was the case,
the situation was threatening peace with Costa Rica.

I read it over quickly and wondered who the
"sources" were and if maybe they were the same people who were responsible for the article on the Medellín cartel of two days before. And I wondered, if
it was the same people, why they were doing it.

There was one other new piece of information. The
police had found Chelly's plane abandoned at a small
dirt airstrip outside the city. The article said there was
nothing in it, but of course there was. Air.

I finished reading, got ready and headed for the
club before noon. It was raining, what the papers said
was the first wave of a tropical storm. When I got to
the club, I went right to the roulette wheel to relieve
my man so he could go to lunch. Old man Soo was
there, a crusty old Chinaman who owned a restaurant
nearby, and I was spinning the ball for him alone.

Pedro came back, but I stayed near the wheel to try
and bring Soo some luck. I was still there and Soo was
playing red and winning, when Akers from the U.S.
embassy walked in. He was wearing a long black rain
poncho. He had pulled the hood back and uncovered
his small head and his sweeping white hair.

"Good afternoon, Colonel," I said to him.

He blinked at me. Then his head swiveled, he
darted a glance around the club and looked back at
me. He said in a courtly way:

"Good afternoon, Mr. Lacey."

Later, another journalist friend who had sources in
the intelligence community gave me some of the de-

tails on Colonel Akers's career. I say "some" because there were periods of time when nobody was sure where he had been or what he was up to. He was quite a fellow, the colonel.

Except for a brief tour of duty in Vietnam in the late sixties, Akers had been on loan from the army to the CIA to perform intelligence and counterinsurgency operations in Latin America for more than thirty years.

He showed up for the first time in 1954 when the CIA helped Guatemalan military officers overthrow the government there, after it tried to confiscate some land from the U.S. fruit companies. It was considered the first big CIA covert operation in the Latin countries, and Akers, a young second lieutenant, just out of West Point, with a bit of Spanish, participated in a significant victory.

"He was off and running," said my journalist friend.

From there Akers began to move all over Latin America, wherever there were problems. He was sent to Colombia in the mid-fifties during the troubles there, was in Havana just before Castro marched in triumphantly in 1959, and then traveled secretly to Guatemala in '61 to train the Cubans of the 2506 Brigade who fought at the Bay of Pigs. It was there that he first met and befriended Cassanova, then only a teenage soldier.

Akers was assigned to Panama in 1963 during the anti-American demonstrations and in 1965 he landed on the shores of the Dominican Republic as part of the Marine incursion. Then he disappeared for a while. It was thought he might have gone to Peru to help neutralize the Aprista movement in the mid-sixties.

"He definitely chased Che Guevara through the

mountains of Bolivia in nineteen sixty-six until they trapped Guevara and killed him," my friend said. "That was a real feather in his helmet."

Then Akers disappeared again until the late sixties when he was transferred to Vietnam for a stint against the Vietcong.

When he returned to Latin America was not certain either, but he was seen in Chile in 1973 when the CIA helped overthrow the socialist government there and the president, Allende, was killed. From there Akers made a move that was to bring him to Central America and keep him there: he was transferred to the military school at Fort Gulick, Panama, where for several years he taught intelligence and counterinsurgency to most of the top military officials of the Central American armies. The journalist told me it was there that Akers formed the network of contacts that he was to use later on in fighting leftist rebels from Salvador and Guatemala and the Sandinistas of Nicaragua.

"It was like a regional army and Akers was the commanding general," my friend said.

Despite his efforts the Sandinistas took over Nicaragua in '79, but within weeks of the defeat, Akers was already beginning to organize the force that would become the Contra army.

And now, as time and resources were running out for the Contras, he had appeared in Costa Rica. He stood blinking at me now, as if he were sending me a message in some kind of code. The message said I wasn't supposed to know he was a military man, but in the long run it didn't matter.

"I'm glad to see you in good health," he said. "You may have heard that yesterday one of our fellow Americans was found dead."

"I've heard."

"I understand he was one of the many who flocked to your club?"

"He came in from time to time. He liked to play the wheel. But I didn't know him well."

He blinked at me some more and shook his head stiffly from side to side.

"It's a crime," he said.

"Yes, it was. It was murder."

"It's a crime what is happening here," he said. He fixed on me now. "I'll tell you, Mr. Lacey, these days I don't like the lay of the land. We are seeing a change in the balance of forces, in the basic conditions for survival in this part of the world, in the very nature of the region. Violence is moving downward into Costa Rica."

He spoke gravely, as if he was talking about a glacier edging south towards us.

The black ball rattled in the wheel and settled into a cup. It attracted Akers's attention. Pedro called black and raked in Soo's chip. The Chinaman muttered under his breath. He looked up at Akers to see who had broken his luck. Akers blinked at him without expression and Soo slapped another chip on the red. Akers turned to me.

"I've been all over these countries, Mr. Lacey, overseeing some of our efforts in the region. I've overflown the countries and walked in the backwoods. I've seen the beauty of Central America." He stopped blinking now and got that same hard, cruel look. He said, "I've also seen some terrible, terrible things."

"I'm sure you have," I said flatly.

He was staring into the distance.

"I've seen fields full of bodies and ground soaked through with blood," he said. "Scorched earth. A horrific landscape."

I was watching him, but I thought of Renard.

"Not the kind you see in *National Geographic*," I said.

He turned and blinked at me a few times.

"I wouldn't like to see it in Costa Rica, Mr. Lacey," he said. "Saigon was once quiet like San José. Of course, then you started getting your destabilization, your sabotage, your bicycle bombs. Then the peaceful nature of the city was transformed."

"I take it you were in Vietnam," I said.

He nodded stiffly.

"A bit," he said. "Just a bit."

The ball rattled and hopped into a cup. Pedro called black and swept in Soo's chip. Soo mumbled something in Chinese and then slapped down a chip on red again.

Akers didn't notice. He was telling me:

"There are people who say we are in another Vietnam here, Mr. Lacey; another quagmire." He swiveled his shoulders to shake his head. "I tell them there are no swamps to get stuck in here in Central America, except for the ones we make for ourselves with moral quibbling."

He smiled now, his lips turning up on either side of his hooked nose.

"I tell them Central America is full of tropical mountains and in them is where we'll find the enemy. We need the stamina to scale those mountains and drive the enemy off. We need to take the high ground."

He was looking at me now.

"But there are always people who insist on getting bogged down in the swamps," he said. "You don't care for swamps, do you, Mr. Lacey?"

I shook him off.

"Too many mosquitoes," I said. "And too many snakes. Although you find snakes too on the high ground."

He smiled and blinked at the distance.

"You must take the high ground, Mr. Lacey. From there, you can look down and see how it all works. You see clearly that survival here involves the use of a healthy instinct and not the abstraction of morality. There are those who expect us to protect our nation's interests without getting our claws dirty. That is impossible."

He blinked into the future and then turned back to me.

"The other side knows this as well, Mr. Lacey. Their leaders and their most effective agents. They keep their sights on their goal." He blinked three times as if he were focusing his own sights. "In fact, you know one of their best agents," he said. "His name is Victor Mena."

The chickens were coming home to roost now. The ball was spinning around the wheel again, but I didn't pay it mind. I sipped my drink and kept from smiling at Akers.

"Yes. I knew him."

"He recruited you to the cause some years back."

"He enlisted me to fight nine years ago, until the war was over. And that's all I did."

He nodded and blinked at me. I asked him:

"Do you know Mena?"

"Only by reputation and very briefly by sight. We've never spoken. But I know he's a very talented man."

I shrugged.

"I wouldn't know."

"I would. He's been a top official in internal security in Nicaragua for the past nine years," Akers said. "During that time the Contras have managed no significant assassinations and very few large acts of sabotage, despite U.S. assistance. There have been very few big scores. They say this is because Mena has agents infiltrated at every level of the Contra army, even the highest. And that he also has agents in the countries where the Contras operate. Honduras and here. His intelligence is excellent."

He was looking at me cleverly as if I was one of these agents.

"Like I said, I wouldn't know."

"You haven't seen him lately, have you?"

I made a face at him.

"I told you last time, I haven't been to Nicaragua in almost nine years."

He shook his head.

"That doesn't matter," he said. "You see, we're positive that Mena is here in Costa Rica."

The ball was rattling again and Soo cursed under his breath.

Chapter

—12—

THAT afternoon there was news on the radio of more trouble up on the border. The reports said the Sandinistas and the Contras were engaged in a large firefight up there, and that some Sandinista mortar fire had crossed into Costa Rican territory. A reporter interviewed the same politicians and they said the country was in the middle of a crisis.

The visit I'd gotten from Colonel Akers was bad news enough. He had stayed a while longer and I'd told him a couple times more that I knew nothing about Victor Mena. He had blinked at me awhile, and I couldn't tell whether he believed me or not. Then he'd taken off.

It was about five in the afternoon when Isla rolled in. She wasn't working that night, so I wondered what she was doing there. She was dressed in clothes that were as much a costume as what she wore in the show. She had on blue short-shorts that made her legs look even longer than they were, red stiletto heels, a halter top with green cloth flowers pinned on her breasts and winged sunglasses with palm trees on them. When she took them off I could see her eyes were puffy and red. It turned out this was the outfit she wore when she was in mourning.

"Chelly he's dead, Jack. I hear it on the radio."

I nodded.

"I heard yesterday."

She just shook her head. Her hair was wet from the rain, she looked washed out from crying.

"Who keel him, Jack?"

"I don't know, baby."

A fresh tear rolled down her brown face.

"Chelly he was very nice to me," she said. "He send me flowers and presents. He was a very beeg fan to me."

I'd seen Isla and the pilot keeping company a few times in the club between shows. It had worried me a bit at the time, because there was only one theme that could exist between them: drugs. I thought about it now. I ordered her a drink and when it came I sat down with her.

"What kind of presents did Chelly send you, baby?"

She looked at me now like an ingenue, the picture of innocence, which wasn't easy for Isla. I leaned towards her.

"Did he send you coke, Isla? Something to keep you going on the rainy days off. You can tell me. I know you don't bring it here."

She was suspicious and a bit scared too. She shook her head, biting her lip. I said to her:

"Somebody killed him. I figured maybe they ripped coke off him. That was the motive."

She was still shaking her head.

"Lately he don't have none, Jack. He have plenty of money, more than he ever have, but he don't have no coke. Maybe they keel him for the money."

"Did he tell you where he got all this money?"

She shook her head again.

"I don't ask somebody that."

Especially somebody like Chelly, I thought.

"Did he ever tell you this story about flying air around? Planes with just air in them."

Now she looked at me as if I was crazy.

"I don't know nothing about air," she said, as if air had suddenly become illegal. "He was always a nice person, Jack."

"Yeah, he was a prince," I told her.

She wiped a tear off her face.

"I'm going to leave Costa Rica, Jack," she said.

I winced at her. It was as if she'd stuck me in the ribs.

"You didn't have anything to do with him getting killed," I said. "Did you?"

She was shaking her head so that her hair flew back and forth.

"But I have to go out of here," she said. "This place it is bad for me now."

I tried to talk her out of it, but finally I saw it wasn't going to be. She was leading a stormy life, Isla, and now it was going to drag her away to someplace else. She said she'd do her last shows over the weekend.

We had a couple of memorial drinks for Chelly, and then Isla offered a toast to us.

"We might have been a beautiful couple, Jack," she said, with the tears for Chelly still in her eyes.

We drank up then and she left.

* * *

About seven o'clock I felt like getting out so I walked downtown to get some dinner. It was drizzling and the neon signs reflected off the wet pavement. The rush hour was over and the streets were quiet.

I turned the corner where the Hotel Guerrero sat. I wasn't seeing much. I was thinking about how Isla was taking a hike on me and who I might get to keep the show going. Ray had a sister who did some singing. She could fill in for a while, although it wouldn't be the same. Or maybe I should sell out, like the Dessert Man had said. Cash in my *cheeps*, go to the Caribbean, buy a boat and fish a couple of years.

I was a block past the Hotel Guerrero, about to turn off to a restaurant nearby, when a car made the corner fast and screeched to a stop in front of the hotel. In a moment, two guys jumped out, assault rifles in their hands. I just had time to dodge into a doorway before they opened up.

For the next twenty seconds the street rattled with the noise of AK-47s. One guy on the opposite side of the street stuck his head out a window to see what the racket was, but ducked back in quick. From the angle I had I saw the glass doors of the Guerrero explode into pieces.

Then one of the guys stepped back, lifted his rifle as if he were a hunter sighting a duck, and shot out windows on the top floor of the hotel, where the Dessert Man had his operations suite. The broken glass fell to the street and shattered, like icicles.

Suddenly, another car made the same corner, not knowing what was happening. One of the gunmen turned in our direction and fired a short burst. The bullets passed far over the car, but the message was clear enough. The driver slammed on the brakes, jammed it into reverse and disappeared out of the scene with a squealing of tires.

It was then the gunmen in the street started to draw return fire. Shots fell at them from the top floor, probably the Elevator Boy or Pepe himself, hiding behind his bar. More shots came from the lobby, the bodyguards behind their potted palms. The two guys in the street jumped back in the car then and it took off fast, disappearing around the next corner. The whole incident had taken about thirty seconds.

Quiet filled the street, as loud as the shooting had been. Then it was broken. Screaming and confusion sounded from the broken windows. A couple of the bodyguards came out of the Guerrero into the street, holding pistols in their hands. I left my doorway then and walked down that way. More people were pouring out of the lobby now and onto the street. By the time I got there, the Dessert Man was out in the street, his pistol wrapped in his fat hand.

He spotted me and looked suspicious.

"What are you doing here, Jack?" he said, waddling towards me.

"I was just out for a quiet stroll," I told him.

He waved his pistol at the shattered doors.

"You see what your friends do?"

I looked at him hard.

"They aren't any friends of mine. And you shouldn't go around saying they are."

But I was thinking even then what Akers had said earlier, that Victor Mena was in town. It didn't seem like Mena's style, too noisy, too sloppy. But I thought about it.

Pepe was still glaring at me, the drizzle gathering on his bald head.

"You see now what is happening here. I told you it would happen."

He was waving the gun again, and I pushed it aside.

"You're gonna shoot somebody," I said.

"It's your friends the Sandinistas," he said now, loud enough for everybody to hear. "Look what they are doing to Costa Rica, to all of Central America. There will not be peace until they are gone. They will sink the whole region into war."

Some of the "consultants" registered at the hotel were out in the street now too and they were standing around us. They were looking at me as if I were a spy behind enemy lines.

Just then a police car made a corner up the street with its siren going and raced towards us. Another came just behind it. Cops poured out of them like out of troop carriers. I stuck around a few minutes. It turned out one of the bodyguards was wounded and a couple of people had been hit by flying glass, but those were the only casualties.

I decided to take off then. There were enough witnesses to this incident, they didn't need me. And I didn't need my name in the paper again.

I turned around and headed back to the club again. I found Ray outside on the steps.

"What's happenin'?" he said. "It sounds like quite a bash 'cross town."

We went inside to my table and I filled him in.

"Somebody tryin' to spoil the party here in San José," Ray said. "And they doin' a good job."

Yes, somebody was. But who and why? I had a drink and then another and thought about it awhile. An hour later, I decided to call Renard. He had been up at the border days before and then he had gone looking for Mr. Cassanova and his friends. Maybe he had come up with something. I'd told him about the phone calls made by Topo, so he owed me.

I called him. It was busy the first few times. Reporters talk a lot. Finally I got through to him around nine o'clock.

"Hello, Jacques," he said. "It's good that you call. I am just back again last night from the north."

I told him then about what I had seen at the Guerrero.

"I just heard a report on the radio," he said. "But you were there and you will tell me, no? I have some hot news for you as well."

"Shoot."

"Over the phone, no. Better you come here to the office. I have someone else who is coming. You come in one hour."

I said I would.

Renard kept a small apartment on the east side of town just across from the big old fort the army used to be in.

It was dark and drizzling when I got there an hour later. By that time the sirens had stopped in the center of town.

I found his car on the street and parked behind it. It had "TV" taped on the windows, the new international symbol for the press in war zones. It was supposed to protect you from the fire of combatants. It seemed strange to see it in Costa Rica, especially in the middle of San José.

I headed up the slate stairs to his place. Across the road, the fortress was silhouetted against the rain clouds, its tower and its high castle walls with spaces at the top for people to shoot arrows at you.

Renard had his business card tacked to the door,

Claude Renard, and the name of his agency. I knocked and waited. There was a radio on inside. A news-reader was giving the account of the trouble up north. It was loud, so I knocked again.

I thought I heard something inside, but he didn't answer. So I tried the door and it opened.

I stepped into the apartment and stopped dead. It looked like a hurricane had hit it. And not Isla Vega, either. The place was two rooms, the office in front and the bedroom behind it. In the office there were newspapers all over the place. The drawers had been pulled out of the grey metal file cabinets and the files were dumped out and the cabinets tipped over. There was a typewriter on the floor and someone had ripped out the back of a portable computer and then thrown it in a corner. Renard had had a few photographs of himself with certain Central American leaders framed and hanging on the wall. Now somebody had ripped the photos out of the frames and the glass was broken. The phone was off the cradle and beeping.

The door leading to the bedroom was open. The lights were on there and I saw clothes on the floor. I called for Renard, but there was no answer. I got to the door and had to step over a file cabinet.

Just as I did it, the door came at me. It caught me on the left shoulder, knocked me over a night table so that I hit the edge of the bed and fell to the floor. As I did, a guy jumped out from behind it, went over the file cabinet and ran towards the front door. All I saw of him was his back and his shirt, a yellow trop-ical with a pattern of big blue flowers.

I turned then and saw Renard lying on the bed. He looked paler than ever. There was a trail of blood coming out of a hole in his neck. It looked like red ink against his white skin. His eyes were wide open as if he had been studying death as it approached so he could write an article about it. He wouldn't ever write it or anything else again.

I got up then, jumped over the file cabinet and went out the door fast. The guy in the print shirt was just hitting the street. I saw him in the glow of the mercury light. He turned, looked up at me and slipped on the wet pavement and went down. That gave me a chance.

He picked himself up and tore down the street, but I took the stairs down three at a time and gained some ground. He ran along the black wrought-iron fence outside the fort, crossed a street and a block away entered a park. I followed him past a big old statue, some people with shields and spears fighting, and saw him sprinting maybe fifty yards ahead of me out of the park and up into the old town.

The streets there were narrow and winding. He led me past other historic landmarks from colonial times and then through a couple of curves where I thought he'd lose me. But on either side the buildings were old, with high stone walls, some of them covered with vines, and there was no place to cut off. An old woman came out of a doorway with an umbrella and I screamed at her to call the police. I kept going. I could hear his shoes on the wet street and when I turned the second corner I could see him ahead of me, running uphill now with no way out.

My legs were longer and I started to gain on him, when suddenly he braked, turned and crouched down. He pulled out a pistol that wasn't from the colonial era at all and fired two shots.

I threw myself into an old arched doorway and smashed my shoulder against a studded wooden door. I stayed still there moments, battling for breath and holding the shoulder. When I peeked around the edge of the doorway he was gone. I ran to the corner but all I saw was an empty street.

I stood gasping for breath as if I was trying to inhale the whole landscape. I hung my head between my knees and after a minute I started walking back to Renard's place in the rain. When I got there I went into the bedroom. Renard was still there. He wasn't going anyplace.

Then I picked up the phone and called Eddie Pasos's office. I told the boy who answered what had happened and to find Eddie. Then I found an unbroken bottle of rum and sat down to wait. It had been quite a night.

Twenty minutes later Eddie arrived with his posse. I pointed him back to the bedroom. He was gone a minute, then he came back and I told him what had happened and gave him a description of my tour guide. Medium height, medium build, dark hair and a tropical shirt. In a place like San José, that was lots of help.

He sent his men out, then he turned to me.

"You always seem to be where we find the dead."

I nodded.

"I put an ad in the paper about ten days ago. 'Let me know if you plan to get killed.' "

I poured myself more rum.

Eddie gazed around the office.

"What do you know about this?"

"I know Renard's tomorrow's news, along with this evening's floor show at the Hotel Guerrero," I said. "The news is getting to be the same every day around here."

Eddie didn't like that analysis of current events and he frowned.

"What do you know about the shooting at the hotel?" he asked.

"It was loud," I said. "Apart from that I don't know anything you don't already have. Did you get the boys who did it?"

He shook his head. "Not yet."

Eddie watched me drink a few moments and then nodded towards the bedroom.

"This man was a reporter."

"That's right."

"What did you come here to talk to him about?"

"I didn't come to talk to him; he was going to talk to me. He said he'd been up at the border and also around town here and he had some hot news."

"And why was he going to report that to you?"

"Because I asked him to check into a few things for me."

"What, for example?"

"For example, why me and my acquaintances have become sport for guys with guns and bombs and nobody does anything about it."

Eddie's stiff upper lip went stiffer.

"Renard was going to find out for me. He had good sources," I said.

"Who were these sources?"

"He didn't say. They were confidential. But I know he was nosing around Pepe Esparza and his boys. There's a lead for you. Go hound *him*. Just because Pepe got shot at tonight doesn't mean he hasn't done his own shooting."

Eddie was kicking aside files and newspapers, picking up loose sheets of paper and letting them drop.

"So you believe maybe the journalist found some information which he shouldn't have, and he was killed."

"He told me somebody was coming to talk to him tonight. I guess that somebody didn't like Renard's questions."

Eddie started to speak, but I cut him off.

"No, I don't know who it was. All I saw was his back—if that was the guy he was going to interview, I don't know."

I sipped more of the rum.

"Now why don't you tell me what you know, Eddie. Your government must know something about this by now."

Eddie shook his head.

"We don't have the good sources of your friend, unfortunately," he said.

He drifted into the bedroom then and I followed him. Renard lay under the sheet in the midst of the rubble of notebooks and newspapers.

"Why would they do this to the office? What information could he have hidden here?" he asked.

"I wouldn't know."

Eddie picked up Renard's wallet, which was lying on the night table. It had been emptied and its contents were strewn on the bed. He picked up Renard's press card issued by his agency years before. It showed him younger, but with the same sharp features and no less cynical. Eddie picked up some of his calling cards and other pieces of paper. A photo of his daughter as well.

I was standing there sipping the rum, staring into nothing. Eddie was saying that they would report Renard's death to the French embassy that same night. Then I saw something, something that leapt out at me. It was written in red ink on one of Renard's calling cards lying on the bed next to the dead man. It said, "Nicaragua, Hill 116."

I picked it up and stared at it, as if it were a phone number where I could reach Renard even in death. I was trying to remember who had talked to me about Hill 116. And then I remembered. Eddie was watching me.

"What do you have there?"

"Topo mentioned this to me the night he was killed. I didn't remember. Hill One-sixteen."

Eddie took the card away from me and stared at it, as if he was trying to break a code.

"What does it mean?" he asked me.

I shook my head.

"I don't know," I said. "Like I told Topo, I wasn't there."

Chapter

—13—

I got back to the club about eleven. I still had the sound of those shots ringing in my ears, and the sight of Renard lying there dead.

Ray was gone for the night, so I took a back table by myself near the doors to the casino. I thought about the job those gunmen had done on the Guerrero and then about Renard. I remembered what the Dessert Man had said: that Topo and Chelly had been killed by the Sandinistas because they had been marked as traitors.

I sipped a drink and for the first time I thought I might have to head for the hills, get out of Costa Rica, at least for a time. I didn't know why it was happening, but I could see clearly enough the connection between me and the three dead men. In fact, as far as I knew, I was the only one who knew all three of them. In the space of a week, they had all been killed.

I had two drinks in honor of Renard. With the third in my hand I drifted back into the casino.

There was only one player at the wheel, the old Chinaman named Soo. He had walked over from his restaurant to gamble some of the receipts he had raked in at lunch. Soo had once offered me a deal: a year's supply of chop suey lunches in exchange for some free chips for roulette. I told him I'd rather not, because his chop suey was a gamble in the first place.

I sat there not as drunk as I should have been, watching Soo play the wheel. I stared at his face, which was smooth for an old man, and his wisp of a goatee. Soo and how he had gotten to Costa Rica was quite a story. It was a story that, given my current situation, had a lot to do with me.

He was born in China, Soo, and was still there in 1947 when Mao Tse-tung was waging his war of revolution. He was young enough to fight, but he couldn't see the odds in going to war and decided to get out of China. So he scraped together a stake, asked around about the best bet for a new homeland, said goodbye to his honorable family and put his young wife and kids on a ship to make his new life. He decided to stay in Asia, not go too far away. He picked a country nearby. Vietnam.

That was before the south blew up, of course, and Soo even had a streak of luck when he first got to Saigon. He found an old Chinaman who wanted to go partners and ended up with a good location for a restaurant in the Cholon district. Soo played the favorites: he mixed a little French and local cooking with the Chinese and that way he attracted colons and middle-class Vietnamese. He decorated the place with cheap watercolors of the Eiffel Tower and the

Champs-Élysées and bad reproductions of Chinese woodcuts.

Soo was sitting pretty for a while. But, of course, a few years later the French got defeated at Dien Bien Phu. They pulled out and then old Ho Chi Minh started sending his boys from up north down into Saigon. Places of business started blowing up all around Soo. The Chinaman cursed his bad luck again, but he didn't have the capital to make another move so he sat tight.

He hung on that way into the sixties and the coming of the Americans. He put a few Yankee dishes on the menu and business started picking up again. But his wife began having disaster dreams and telling him they had to get out. Soo studied maps and talked to other Chinamen. The U.S. and Europe sounded nice, but there were too many Chinese restaurants there already. He considered Africa too and Canada. Then one day in a gambling joint he heard from a Chinese seaman about a cheap fare on a freighter heading for Panama. As far as Soo was concerned fate had spoken. He decided he would get to Panama and then toss a coin to determine whether he went north or south in Latin America.

He dragged his family up the gangplank and the ship lifted anchor. It happened that working down in the laundry of the ship he found some Chinamen who had been around Latin America. They told him about a country where he should go, a real land of opportunity for Chinamen. Where there were few Chinese restaurants and a wealthy land-owning class that would pay well for egg rolls. He couldn't miss. The place was Nicaragua.

War drove Soo out of Nicaragua as well, of course,

and he had come to Costa Rica about four years ago.
Now he sat over the wheel staring at it as it spun,
with that sour look, as if the wheel would measure for
him just how unlucky he was. Which was valuable
knowledge. Or maybe it was lucky. He had been
through all that and was still alive. Maybe that's what
I should be thinking about, staying alive.

I came out of the casino, went back to my table,
ordered another drink. The place was almost empty
and I sat looking at it and thinking things over. I was
still there after midnight when I saw her come through
the door. She was wearing a short black leather jacket
and jeans. She looked around, spotted me and came
over. She sat down in the chair next to me and stayed
looking at me with a serious expression. The jacket
and her hair were wet with the rain.

"You're out late," I told her. "Did you feel lucky
and decide to play the wheel awhile?"

"I just heard on the radio about the killing of the
French journalist," she said. "I know he was a friend
of yours."

I'd had a few drinks already and I was slouched in
the chair. I was a bit drunk, but still viable. I took
another pull at the drink.

"We knew each other," I said.

She nodded, that same serious look on her face.

"It's very difficult to lose a friend that way, so suddenly."

I shrugged.

"It's happened before." I was thinking then of Carlos and how he had been killed in the insurrection.

"Still it is difficult no matter how many times it
happens," she said.

I didn't answer that. In the background Nina Simone was singing something soothing and sad about lost love.

She fiddled with a swizzle stick and asked me:

"Was he married?"

"Several times. He'll be mourned by women on various continents."

"Did he have children?"

"One, a daughter. Sixteen. She got a bad deal."

She drank that in and I drank more of my rum.

"So what brings you here at this hour?" I asked her. "Do you want a report on this killing like you did on Topo Morales? I didn't catch the last words this time. He was already dead when I got there. He had no tip to give me."

She shook her head.

"I just came to see you," she said in a husky whisper.

My eyebrows must have registered some surprise.

"You came to comfort me?" I said, and it sounded cynical, but she just stared at me.

Some of the last customers drifted out then and I watched them go out the door. I turned back and she was still looking at me.

"The radio reported they killed him in his apartment," she said. "Did they break in to kill him? Do you know?"

"He was waiting for somebody, and he let them in himself," I said. I tasted my drink and looked at her, the wet coat and hair. I thought to myself: Of course, if it was a woman who came to the door, a good-looking woman, he would have let her in without question. Renard had healthy instincts. Or at least I thought they were healthy. Now he was dead.

She was frowning at me as if she could hear what

I was thinking. But she didn't say anything. She acted as if she were dealing with a disturbed personality, someone who had to be handled with care.

She rolled the swizzle stick in her fingers.

"Did your friend ever tell you he was afraid someone would kill him?"

"No."

"Can you think of anyone who would want to kill him?"

"Yeah, lots of people," I said. "He was a trouble-maker. He also knew lots of things he wasn't supposed to know about lots of people. Inside information."

I gave her a pointed look as if some of it might be about her and her colleagues at the embassy.

She squinted at me.

"Did he say he thought my government might want to harm him?"

"No, he didn't," I said. "He didn't mention anybody, but there was somebody who wanted him dead, wasn't there?"

She stared hard at me now as if she were trying to read the marks on the back of a crooked deck. Then she said:

"If we can assure that you will find out who killed your friend, will you do something for us?"

That's how she put her cards on the table. I watched her to determine if in fact it had been her and her friends who killed Renard and she was trying to bluff me. She let me look into her eyes, but she wasn't giving anything away.

"How do I know it wasn't you guys who killed him," I said.

She shook me off. "Because it wasn't."

"And why should I buy what you tell me? Why should I take the risk?"

"Because what we would ask you to do would not be illegal or extremely dangerous and you would find out who killed the Frenchman. It would be a gamble with little risk."

"And what would this gamble consist of?"

She shook her head.

"I don't hold that information yet," she said. "And now is not the time to discuss it."

I had to smile then.

"That's right," I said, "you weren't here to discuss business. You were here to comfort me." I sipped my drink. "So how does that go?"

She glanced at me from behind that tree of hers. Then she raised the ante. She leaned over the table like a player who was about to rake in a pot she'd won, put a hand up to my cheek and kissed me on the lips. It was a good kiss, not everything she had, but enough.

When she finished she pulled back and looked at me, like maybe she'd gone too far, bet too much. She waited to see if I would see her bet and maybe raise it, but I didn't. Not that she wasn't tempting, but it wasn't the moment to get involved in that game. She pursed her lips then, as if she was putting them away for the night, and stood up.

"I'm sorry about your friend."

I nodded to her.

"We will see each other before long," she said, and she turned and went out.

I watched her leave. I sat and finished my drink. Then I closed the place down and took myself home.

Chapter

—14—

I was dreaming again, but this time it was a real nightmare.

I was walking down a dark hallway. I found myself outside the apartment where I had grown up. I turned the key, opened the door and found the hallway I recognized. But I also found a body sprawled in the hall, a dark-haired young soldier dressed in camouflage. I knew at a glance he was dead.

I went by him into the living room. The small room was exactly as I remembered it, the same worn furnishings, the same feel of the city. But now it was full of dead. Ten, twenty, bodies. Some were in camouflage, some were civilians. They were all lying on their stomachs and I couldn't see the faces. There was complete silence. I stopped to turn one over, but just then the sound of shooting came from outside. I went to the window, looked down and found the same street I'd grown up on, but now covered with bodies. All faceless dead. From somewhere nearby, I could still hear shooting. One era in my life had invaded an earlier one. Or maybe the dream was telling me you can't go back again.

Then suddenly I heard people coming up the stairs, the sound of footsteps and voices. I froze. Somehow I knew they were coming to kill me. There was no place to go. I looked at the dead, lowered myself to the floor and laid down with them. I held my breath and waited, but no one came. The shooting outside had stopped. All I could hear was the total silence of the dead and feel how still and how dead they were. I felt as if I was falling like them into death.

I woke with a start and sat up in bed. It was day, but completely quiet in the house. I got up quickly and went to the kitchen where I found Jacoba. She was alive, but not happy. She was talking to God about how the world was coming to an end. She shoved the papers at me. They were just an extension of the nightmare. "Violence Explodes in Capital," "Terrorists Attack San José." There was a short article on the death of Renard they had gotten in at the last moment. It didn't mention me; this time Eddie had kept me out of it.

Then the phone rang. It was Ray.

"We missin' a bartender and a croupier," he said. "The rats are leavin' the ship."

"I'll be there," I told him.

I got ready and was down there quick. A few customers stood at the bar drinking, as if they were trying to forget what was happening around them in San José. For the next few hours I manned the dice table in the casino. Then about six o'clock one of the boys came in to tell me there were some gentlemen outside looking for me.

When I came out of the casino they were sitting
there. Cassanova, Paraiso and the other guerrilla boy
I had seen in the Dessert Man's hotel suite. They were
at a table across the way, all of them sitting so they
didn't give their backs to the door and all of them
looking right at me.

Chico came over to me.

"These *señores* would like to talk to you," he said.
Chico had worked in the place a long time and was
used to some of the rough trade we got at times, but
even he looked a bit edgy when he glanced at them.

"Bring me a drink," I told him, and I went over.

Cassanova stood up to greet me with a smile and a
handshake. He was polite and polished, like many of
the military men I'd met over the years in Central
America. It didn't keep them from being lethal when
they felt like it. If you looked closely, the smile was
all teeth. The eyes stayed as cold as the ice in one of
the drinks on the table.

"It is a pleasure to meet you, Mr. Lacey. My name
is Raul Cassanova."

"Pleasure," I said, although that was the last thing
it was. The other two boys weren't in his class. They
sat glaring at me with their muddy eyes, doing their
best to look menacing. They were doing all right
at it.

Cassanova gestured to a chair but I shook him off.

"No thank you," I said.

He sat down, kept his smile on and nodded. He had
a deep tan, as if he spent a lot of time working on it.
The only spot that wasn't dark brown was a round
scar on his temple, in the shape of a sunburst, as if
maybe he'd been hit with a bullet. He was wearing a
tropical shirt with vines crawling through the pattern.
He wore it unbuttoned halfway down his chest so the

black chest hairs showed. He was a work of nature, Raul Cassanova.

He had worked on his muscles too, and he had a lot of them. While he talked he was constantly craning his muscular neck, rocking his head back and forth, kneading his forearms. I thought about Topo and Chelly and Renard too. This crew sitting in front of me could have killed them easy.

"What can I do for you?" I asked.

Cassanova stretched his neck and then looked at me.

"I am thinking of going into business here," he said with his Cuban accent, "and Mr. Esparza he tells me maybe you want to sell this place."

I frowned.

"Where did he get that idea?"

"He said maybe you were worried now because of the trouble in San José these days. The violence," Cassanova said, and he drank from a highball. "He tells me you knew these people who are killed. Morales and the pilot."

"That's right," I said. "I knew Claude Renard too. He was killed last night, but you already knew that, didn't you?"

Cassanova's smile disappeared and his brow furrowed, as if he was trying to remember who Renard was so he could remember if he had anything to do with killing him. Then his nostrils flared and his eyes went even colder. The other two boys stirred, like watchdogs who'd caught a whiff of something.

"I don't know anything about it," Cassanova said flatly. He was scowling at me as if I had violated the etiquette of this situation. When a man came to drink in your club, you didn't try to accuse him of murder. And I wondered then, if he had killed Renard, would he come the next day to see me.

He was still scowling up at me.

"The Sandinistas must have killed him," he said. "Maybe he discovered that they killed the other two."

"Did they?"

He squinted up at me as if trying to make me smaller in his vision and he nodded.

"I say so."

My *mojito* came then. I sipped it.

Cassanova was shaking his head.

"It is very bad," he said, and he looked sad. "Too many people already dead in Central America. And for Costa Rica maybe this is only the beginning."

"Somebody else was telling me that just yesterday. Colonel Akers from the American embassy."

"Meester Akers," he said with emphasis, "is a very smart man. He has seen very much. I trust his judgement. Maybe you should do so as well."

"Well, then I'll have to consider selling," I said.

The other two boys were listening intently, although you knew they couldn't understand a word we were saying. They were looking for a sudden move in order to leap.

"When you decide to sell, I hope you will give me and Mr. Esparza a chance to make the last offer." He didn't say if, he said when.

"The Dessert Man is your partner," I said.

"That is right. He is a good man, a good businessman, and he knows this part of the world," he said. His gaze sharpened then. "Especially, he knows the Sandinistas, what criminals they are. They are like Castro. They brought his ideas to Central America. They have spread his plague."

He looked at me for confirmation, but I just looked back.

"They took Esparza's land, his and other friends of

171

ours," he said. "But he will get his revenge and we will see that there is justice." He paused a moment for emphasis. "We are working to bring democracy to Nicaragua and people shouldn't get in the way, Mr. Lacey."

I didn't like the sound of that. I was still thinking of Renard lying there dead and now I had these apes walking into my place and trying to put the chill on me. It ticked me off. So I sipped my drink and said:

"I guess it depends what you mean by democracy. Some people around here want democracy only if their section of it is air conditioned and the help doesn't get too uppity. If democracy doesn't go their way, then people get killed."

It wasn't a smart thing to say right then, but it came out.

Cassanova stopped his stretching and flexing, and stayed staring at me. Only his jaw was working as if he was grinding something between his back teeth. The silence between us and the look in his eye made my stomach clench. It was as if some force was working its way through him and at any moment he might come at me. You didn't argue with a man whose whole life, from the time he had been a boy, had been built around one simple and violent article of faith.

It took a few moments for him to regain his equilibrium. It was like watching Mr. Hyde turn back to Dr. Jekyll. He sipped his daiquiri and then put it down. When he spoke his voice was calm and he made a statement of faith.

"Many people have died in Central America, it has been very tragic," he said. "It would not have happened if Castro and his friends had not tried to infect this part of the world with their illness. That has been the cause of the violence. It is like in the human body," he said, jabbing himself in the chest. "It is the natural reaction to the infection he and his friends have brought here. It fights until the body is cured."

"So violence is healthy," I said. "I guess that depends on which side of it you're on."

He looked at me a few moments and then said:

"That's exactly right, Mr. Lacey. It does depend what side you are on." Then he tipped his glass back and finished his drink.

They paid and got up.

"We will see each other again," Cassanova said cordially. And then they went out.

Chapter

—15—

I sat, finishing my drink. What I had been thinking about before was getting out of Costa Rica and nothing Cassanova had said to me had made me change my mind. If anything, a character like Cassanova being around was enough reason to get out. On the other hand, I didn't appreciate being leaned on.

After a while, Ray came in and sat down with me. We had a drink to the memory of Renard.

"He was a good one," Ray said.

"He was all right."

"What's happenin' here, Jack?"

I shook my head. Then I said I was thinking of disappearing for a while and if I did, I would put him in charge of the place. While I was gone, the profits would be his.

"You get a little jumpy, boss," he said.

"What about it?"

"I think maybe it's a good idea, a healthy idea," he said. "Maybe you should leave tonight. And I don't want the profits. I'll still take care of the place."

"We'll see," I told him.

I finished my drink then and I headed home before I had too many to get there.

I had the jeep parked out in front of the door and the guard was right there. So I didn't have to worry about a bomb like the one that carried off Topo. Although with the image of Renard still in my mind, I thought about it when I turned the key.

Then when I got out of town and started hitting the dark curves heading to my place, I found myself staring into the vegetation along the side of the road, thinking of another ambush. I drove the curves quicker than I usually did, like there was somebody chasing me. Ray was right, I was getting jumpy.

I got through them and pulled in at the house. It was just midnight. The light was on, but then Jacoba always left it burning for me. I locked the jeep and headed for the door and that's when I heard someone behind me. I turned quickly and saw this guy step out of the bushes maybe six feet from me. I recognized him right away, it was the dark fellow who had danced that night in the club with Lucia Lara. Here he was straight from the Nicaraguan embassy and I didn't think he was on any kind of diplomatic mission or was going to ask me to dance.

I braced myself and waited for him to come or to get sight of his gun so I could go for it. I thought for a split second of my own pistol lying under the mattress, useless. If I'd had it then I would have used it, I wouldn't have waited or asked questions either.

I braced myself, but I didn't see a gun and he didn't come. He just stood there with his hands up showing me there was no weapon in them. That's when I felt someone else at my back. I turned quickly, expecting to feel the bullet burn into me or the knife prick me, and saw the other embassy boy who had been at the club that night. He didn't have a weapon either, at least not in sight.

Then the front door opened. When I looked she was standing there in the light that fell from over the doorway. She was wearing a tight black skirt and black blouse. I guess it was her nighttime burglary outfit.

"Good evening," she said. She stood watching me with that sly look of hers. I didn't have to ask the usual question this time. She told me.

"This time we picked the lock," she said.

I could feel my heart beat in my chest. For a moment, seeing her, I felt relief. But there was no reason I should. The first time I had seen her, I had expected her to pull a pistol from her briefcase and shoot me neatly and quickly. Since that morning, two other people had been killed. But at least now I knew there would be some foreplay before they did it.

"I wouldn't expect you to wait outside for me," I told her. "It isn't your style."

She stepped back and invited me in and I said thank you. The two embassy boys stepped back. I walked into the house and then I noticed there was another person there. The parrot cage was standing just outside the door that led to the garden and a man stood next to it with his back to me, playing with Ollie. He turned around then. It was Victor Mena.

"Hello, Jack," he said. "It is good to see you again."

He stepped into the room, stopped and looked me over from top to bottom.

"I thought I wouldn't recognize you, but you look the same, you look good. Almost the same as when you were fighting."

Mena didn't look much different either, given it had been nine years. He was a tall, broad man, with handsome mestizo features, and deep-set black eyes. With his size and looks, he had a reputation as a womanizer. The hair was a bit greyer and there were a few more wrinkles in the olive-skinned face, but the black eyes were the same.

"You're looking well yourself, Victor," I said, and I walked to the bar to pour myself a drink. "A couple of times over the years I heard you were dead."

He shrugged.

"It is when people think you are dead that you are the healthiest," he said. "At least in my work."

I smiled at him over the edge of my glass. If Akers was your mythical CIA agent come to life, then Victor Mena embodied the legend of the Latin revolutionary. He was born in Nicaragua, but his parents went into exile during the Somoza years and he spent his childhood bouncing around Latin America. It was in Mexico in 1956, at the age of nineteen, that he found his life's work. Already involved in leftist politics, Mena met up with some young Cubans who were plotting to overthrow the Batista government. Their leader was Fidel Castro. Mena joined up and fought the next two years in the Cuban Sierra Maestra. After Havana fell, Mena was assigned to the foreign affairs department of the Cuban Communist Party. Over the next fifteen years he had contact with revolutionary movements all over Latin America, sometimes traveling under diplomatic cover to make contact with fighters in the mountains. Somewhere along the line he had been wounded in the leg. Maybe in Uruguay, Colombia or El Salvador. It wasn't known.

Finally, in 1974 he went to Costa Rica to join his Nicaraguan compatriots in their war against Somoza and with his experience soon became a top intelligence official. That's how I met him in '78.

He stood there watching me.

"You don't seem particularly surprised to see me, Jack."

"Nothing surprises me anymore," I said.

Mena's mouth made a smile.

"Like a good guerrilla, always prepared for anything," he said. "You were very good, Jack. That is always the intelligence I received about you. Very smart, very courageous. It made me feel good about my own judgement, that it was I who recruited you."

"That was a long time ago," I said. "I'm over the hill as a guerrilla, Victor."

He nodded.

"Yes, we are all over the hill. Especially me." He tapped his bum leg. "I'll never work in the mountains again. But there are other jobs to be done."

He went to the couch now, moving with a pronounced limp. He sat down and said:

"You should have stayed with me, Jack. I could have used you in state security. But I understand why you didn't stay at the time. And I want you to know that I appreciate that you have never been actively disloyal—not like some of the others who happened to work with us during the insurrection."

I didn't say anything to that, although it was clearly a reference to the fallen comrades, Topo and Chelly. She had stayed leaning against a corner near the door and I could feel her eyes on me. Then Mena said:

"Jack, you don't look surprised to see me or very pleased either."

I shook my head.

"A friend of mine was killed last night," I said. "A French journalist, Claude Renard."

Mena's eyes reflected concern. But I couldn't tell if it was my concern or his own. I couldn't tell how much he knew.

"I read about it," he said. "Who do you think killed him?"

I shrugged.

"I don't know. They didn't leave a note. But Renard was looking into recent events here."

Mena was watching me, the wheels turning behind the eyes.

"Like the bombing of Topo Morales and the shooting of the American pilot."

"That's right."

Out in the garden the insects were pulsing and so was the blood through my temples. Right then I was thinking of Renard. If it was Mena who had killed the Frenchman, I wanted to slit his throat. He watched me carefully, as if he could sense what I was thinking. Then he gazed past me and talked as if he was seeing something happening out on the dark hillside and he was describing it to me.

"You know, Jack, when a government becomes involved with secret wars, clandestine operations, it enters a territory that is very unpredictable. There are many unknown and dangerous factors waiting for you."

He looked at me and nodded, his expression somber.

"We ourselves learned this during the insurrection," he said. "In order to arm ourselves and to gather intelligence, we had to involve ourselves with certain people who dealt in these commodities. These collaborators were people who already lived outside the law, they already were involved in criminal activity. Do you know what I mean?"

He looked at me now, the old professor in guerrilla warfare and me the fresh recruit.

"You had to deal with gunrunners and other black market people," I said.

"Exactly," he said. "This American pilot Chelly, he was one of them. He was a mercenary. Whoever paid him, he supported. He flew what they wanted where they wanted. No questions asked. Topo Morales was another. He was already a spy. We didn't turn him into a spy. He was already a very dishonest, untrustworthy man. And there were others in Nicaragua, here in Costa Rica and in other countries, of the same type."

He gestured towards me with a smile.

"Not all our collaborators were as noble and selfless as you."

"Or maybe foolish," I said.

Mena didn't respond. He stayed talking into the garden.

"Of course, when you deal with that kind of criminal collaborator you take certain risks," he said. "You can never be quite sure exactly what they are planning. They may collaborate with you on a certain operation, provide you with a certain product or a service which you need, but they may also have their own motives, their own business. They may involve you in something in which you did not intend to become involved."

He stopped and glanced at me as I sipped my rum. I said:

"Like if you want arms, but they want to run drugs as well."

He nodded.

"That is one example," he said. "There is another problem as well with these collaborators. That is, once you become involved with them, you know something you can use against them, but they also have something they can use against you. And you must assume that they some day will have reason to use it. As their operations change, their allegiances change. You must know they did not survive in that criminal world without being treacherous."

He got up then, limped to the garden door and looked out. I sipped my rum. If this was a eulogy for Topo and Chelly it was quite a send-off, not that either of them deserved much better. About Renard, he had said nothing. I thought then that maybe he was confessing to having eliminated the other two. And if he had killed them, then I figured he had killed the Frenchman too, no matter what he said. But he went in a different direction.

"Both of them, Topo Morales and the American, they were not dependable people," he said. "Lately they had done work for the Contras and I can understand fully why the Contras would want them dead."

His voice was flat and cold as if he was talking about ciphers, about a problem that had to turn out a certain way and not about human beings.

"So the Contras killed them."

He shrugged.

"I assume."

He looked at me blankly, letting me examine his face. It was full of indifference, as if he were saying, you can believe or not, I don't care.

He said:

"We know you have not been disloyal in the way those other two were, Jack. That is why we're coming to you now."

There was just a hint of menace in the voice—it said I better not be disloyal now.

"What is it you want?"

He came over to the bar then, and sat as if he was going to order a drink, his hands folded in front of him.

"There is a situation we need taken care of, Jack, an operation to be carried out," he said. "Believe me, we know you did very much already during the insurrection and we would not ask you unless it was absolutely necessary."

I had the glass halfway to my mouth, but I had to stop and smile. Mena pulled a face.

"What is humorous, Jack?"

I shook my head, sipped my rum and then gestured in her direction.

"Ever since you sent your girlfriend to scout me, I've been expecting this," I said. "I can see that she's spent a lot of time with you, Victor. She doesn't miss a beat when she lies. And even if you know she's lying, she sucks you in with her emotion, her passion. She's very good."

I looked at her then. She was fixed on me from across the room.

Mena looked at her also and then back to me.

"What we want you to do, Jack, will not involve violence, only your knowledge of the people now in San José, only your contacts. In your own way you have infiltrated the society here, you know everyone. And with that knowledge you can help us."

I sipped my rum.

"And just what is it you want me to do?" I asked.

Mena picked up a swizzle stick, rolled it in his
fingers.

"I want you to arrange for a meeting between myself and Colonel Akers," he said.

That caught my attention and he noticed.

"I want you to get in touch with him and tell him
that I want to see him tomorrow night, at this same
time, here," he said. "I want you to tell him he should
come and bring his colleagues Mr. Esparza and Mr.
Cassanova."

I frowned at him.

"And what's to keep you from killing him when he
shows up?" I said.

"If I wanted to kill him, I would send people to kill
him who are in that business," he said. "Anyway, my
government would certainly be blamed for his killing
and it would cause tremendous troubles. I don't want
him dead."

"Or what's to keep Akers from calling the Costa
Rican authorities and having you arrested. Or better
yet, what's to keep them from coming here to kill you,
and me for that matter."

He shook his head, but his black eyes stayed on me.

"They will not do that, Jack. All you have to tell
Akers is one other thing. You tell him we know about
Hill One-sixteen."

I tried to keep from looking surprised and I guess I
just looked confused. Mena said:

"Do you understand? Hill One-sixteen. If you tell
him that, he will come and then you will maybe re-
ceive an explanation of these past days."

I had a picture of Renard in my head, lying there
with the blood coming out of him and the note in red
ink on his bed.

"And how about who killed the Frenchman?" I asked him. "When do you explain that to me."

Mena nodded.

"Tomorrow night you will know. I believe Colonel Akers himself will tell you who killed the Frenchman. And when he tells you, you will believe him."

We looked at each other then. I could see myself in Mena's black eyes, as black as two eight balls.

Outside, the garden was pulsing. I thought how I didn't want to be out in the middle of nowhere with these people.

"I doubt if they would come here. It's isolated, too dangerous," I said.

He didn't seem disturbed.

"Then where would you say?"

I shrugged.

"At the club," I said. "If it's like you say, that there won't be any violence, that's the best place. Right in the middle of town."

"That's fine, Jack," he said. "You tell them at your club after it closes."

He got up then.

"I better disappear again into the night, Jack. Our car is back out through the garden on the side road." He nodded towards her and she went to get the embassy boys. Mena took my arm then.

"If you care to believe me, there is nothing anymore between Lucia and I. There has not been for years. Also, in the beginning she was under orders from her ambassador, not from me, to ask you certain questions."

I didn't say anything and he shrugged. "You can believe that if you please. It is true. At any rate, we will see you tomorrow night."

She came back then with the bodyguards. Mena shook my hand and then he and the guards went out the garden door and disappeared up the dark path. She didn't leave. She stood watching them until the vegetation swallowed them. I said to her:

"I'm surprised you're not leading them out. You snuck in here that way once. You know the way."

She stayed staring into the garden. When she spoke her voice was husky, as if it were muffled by the mist that was just starting to fall into the trees.

"I really didn't know at first that they were going to involve you," she said. "It was like you said. I only knew as much as I needed to know."

"So Victor told me."

I went into the bar then, poured myself a rum, and I poured one for her as well. She had gone to sit on the patio looking out at the hillside, and we drank there together.

"He told me you were only asked to talk to me, to question me about what I knew about Topo. I'm not sure I believe that, but now it doesn't matter."

"It is true," she said.

"And I figure you're staying here to keep an eye on me," I said. "Victor wants to make sure I don't have a change of heart. You're in charge of that. But that doesn't really matter either. Here's to the success of the operation."

I touched her glass with mine and we drank. Then those green-brown eyes of hers were on me.

"I'm not here only because Victor wants me to be," she said.

"Is that right? You mean that's one reason, but not the only one."

Up above Conchita gibbered, as the mist fell into her tree like a blanket.

"Yes," she said. "I told them the first time we met that you were a man pretending to be someone else. That the man known during the insurrection was still in you."

I leaned back in my chair and looked at her.

"It's like Victor always told me," I said. "Sooner or later you walk into an ambush yourself."

She squinted again as if she were taking a bead on me.

"You'll survive," she said with assurance.

"We'll see. Now that I'm a collaborator you might tell me more of what's going on here."

She shook her head.

"You should only tell a collaborator what it is necessary for him to know," she said. "You must know that yourself. Anything more puts him in danger."

"Then how are we going to collaborate?"

She sipped her drink. She was wearing that same bemused look she'd had when I had first seen her standing above the hammock.

"You will perform specific tasks you are given," she said. "And not ask questions."

"I see. And besides setting up meetings, what other tasks do you want me to perform?"

She cocked her head.

"Oh, there are needs that arise," she said.

"Needs."

"Urgent needs. Anytime of the day or night, you must be ready."

"I'm always ready," I said.

She nodded, a sly look in her eyes.

"Yes, I can see that."

Then Conchita started chattering louder, pacing back and forth on a eucalyptus limb.

"Are these tasks dangerous? Conchita only gets like that if there is danger or if she's jealous."

She watched me.

"There may be some danger."

"So how do I protect myself?"

"We'll have to teach you."

"Are you going to teach me that?"

"Yes, I can be your instructor."

"Does that include hand-to-hand combat?"

She squinted at me from behind her tree.

"Not usually," she said, "but it may in this case."

We were sitting very close and I leaned towards her and gave her a kiss, like the one she'd given me the day before, but more so. When I was finished, she pulled back and traced a red fingernail across the back of my hand.

"And we'll have to teach you how to avoid ambushes."

"I have a tendency for falling into them," I said.

She turned and gave me that sly look of hers, as if she was lying in wait for me right then. Those green-brown mountain eyes of hers. Me, I could see the ambush coming a mile away, but I kept going and fell right into it.

I woke up in the middle of the night, thinking I heard something outside. She was lying next to me in the bed, breathing shallowly.

I got up and went out to the garden door, but I didn't see anyone. Conchita was sleeping in the tree above me and Ollie's cage was covered. Maybe it had been a possum or a raccoon. Or maybe it was one of Mena's guards left out there to post watch.

I sat naked on the patio chair staring into the night, smelling the bougainvillea, as if I was posting guard. I sat thinking of what Mena had told me and I thought about Hill 116 and Chelly flying air. And then about Renard and the girl with the pigtails.

And then I tried to figure out just who was hiding inside who. Inside Mena. Inside myself. I sat there until almost dawn. When I had it figured out just what I was going to do, I went to bed.

Chapter

—16—

WHEN I woke up the next day, she had already made her exit. All that was left of her was a trace of lipstick on the sheet, powder on the sink and the dark lines under my eyes.

I went out, sat on the patio, looked out over the tropical scenery and wondered how much longer I'd get to see it. Jacoba brought me some coffee and gave me a meaningful glance. She had probably seen Ms. Lara leave the premises, shortly after dawn. The same woman who had snuck onto the property a few days before. She didn't like it, Jacoba. If I'd told her what I had gotten myself involved in she would like it even less.

At noon, I picked up the phone, called the Hotel Guerrero and had them put me through to the Dessert Man. I told him to meet me around three o'clock at the club, that I had something very important to discuss with him.

"I hope it *is* important, Jack. I don't like to go out

in public these days. It is very dangerous. You have heard about the French journalist who was killed."

"Yes," I said, "but don't worry. You come to the club and you'll get your money's worth." He said he'd manage to get there and I hung up.

Then I read the paper, all the grisly details of Renard's death, including the chronology I'd given Eddie about when I'd called him and when I'd found the body. Except, once again, my name wasn't mentioned. Eddie had kept me out of it, which was a good thing because if I was going to be organizing that meeting, I didn't need newspaper reporters taking up my time. I owed Eddie a couple of favors now.

There was also a brief interview with the French ambassador, who said he expected the authorities to quickly find who had killed Renard and bring the person or people to justice. That meant there would be extra pressure on Eddie just now from his own government.

I showered, got dressed then and headed for the club. I got there around two and found the house about half full for lunch. I went into the office and did a review of the books. If I was going to leave the place to Ray for a while—or forever—I wanted things to be in order.

The club had pretty much cleared out by three o'clock and the boys from the Caribbean Current, Isla's band, were already setting up, when the Dessert Man arrived. We picked up a couple of drinks at the bar and then I took him back to the office. He sank down on the couch and sipped his daiquiri.

"I see you have the show on tonight, Jack," the fat man said. "I hear in the radio that Isla Vega this is her last show here."

I opened the desk drawer, pulled out three comple-
mentary tickets and handed them to him.

"Come see her," I said, "and bring Colonel Akers
and Cassanova with you."

His fat fingers reached for the tickets.

"I will invite them," he said, "although I don't believe Colonel Akers is a big fan of salsa."

I nodded.

"You tell the colonel to come anyway," I said. "The
big show will come afterwards."

The Dessert Man raised his sparse eyebrows.

"What is the attraction?"

"Victor Mena."

Now the fat man's head bobbed on the coils of his
fat neck. He was smiling, although in his eyes there
was nothing but suspicion.

"He is making a special appearance here?"

"Let's just say I know where he's going to be after
midnight tonight. He wants to meet with you, Akers
and Cassanova."

Pepe just breathed, his whole body rising and falling with each breath, as if he was trying to inflate
himself and fill the room.

"He told you that himself?"

I nodded.

"Face-to-face, just last night," I said. "I know Mena
and it's him. Not just somebody pretending."

"So he *is* here."

"Like I said, we had a dialogue."

"But tonight is too soon, Jack. We need more time."

I shook my head.

"It has to be tonight. After tonight, he leaves town."

Now Pepe was shaking his head, but still keeping
his beady chocolate-drop eyes on me.

"I don't like this, Jack. Colonel Akers he will not like it either. He does not care for surprises."

I nodded.

"Yes. I know the colonel doesn't like to play around," I said. "So you tell him that Mena wants to talk about Hill One-sixteen."

The fat man sat without making a move now, as if all three hundred pounds of him perched there on the couch was trying to hide, or stay perfectly still so I wouldn't notice him. Then he licked his lips.

"Hill One-sixteen."

"That's right," I said. "That's the theme Mena wants to discuss. You tell Akers."

A bead of sweat had started rolling from his temple down over his fat cheek. He put on a nervous smile now.

"Why should we do this, Jack?" he said. "Maybe you are selling us out. How do we know you are not setting us up for our enemies?"

"Why would I do that, Pepe? I wouldn't be able to show my face again in San José and I have interests here. Besides, this is your turf much more than it is Mena's. He'd never be able to hit you here and get away."

He sipped his daiquiri, and rehearsed the scene in his head.

"Anyway, that's the deal," I said. "If Akers wants to discuss Hill One-sixteen it has to be tonight. You take whatever security precautions you need."

Pepe finished his drink and hauled himself up off the couch in a hurry to get away.

"I'll see you at ringside tonight," I told him.

"We will come to the show," he said, although I wasn't sure which show he was talking about. Then he waddled out.

*　*　*

194

I went out then myself and made sure everything was being prepared for the night crowd. Given the trouble we'd had the week before, I'd told Ray to bring in two extra bouncers, just to discourage any hijinks. He told me they would be at the club on time. I made sure we had the seafood on ice. With the tropical storm coming, the coast would be in disarray and there might not be fresh stuff coming for a couple of days, so we wanted to make sure we didn't let any spoil. I looked it all over quickly.

Then I told Ray I was heading out to get a meal. I walked down towards the center of town as if I was going to Soo's, but instead I cut off and quickly walked the five blocks towards Eddie Pasos's office. At one point I went around a block once, just to make sure I wasn't being followed. I wasn't.

The uniformed guard outside gave me a quick once-over and I went to the reception desk and they sent me up. The secretary led me in and Eddie offered me a chair. Behind the desk, on the wall, hung an old Remington shotgun. Eddie had told me about it: it was the one his father had used during the anti-army rebellion of 1948.

Eddie was in complete uniform. He preened his moustache and rocked back in his swivel chair.

"We have known each other about eight years, Jack, and this is the first time you have ever appeared in my office," he said. "What can I do for you?"

"You can come to my place after midnight tonight," I told him. "There is going to be a little meeting staged there that will interest you."

Eddie rocked in his chair and worked on his moustache.

"That is a little late for a meeting," he said. "Who will be there? What is it about?"

"The characters who killed Topo Morales, Chelly the pilot and Claude Renard," I said. "Nicaraguans, from both sides of the fence, both sides of the war."

Eddie stopped rocking and considered me very seriously. I said to him:

"You get there around two o'clock and they will be there in their seats. They and nobody else. I'll close the house early. My information is these people will be able to tell you who has done all the killing. And given the pressure you're getting from the French ambassador and people in your own government, that would be a good thing."

Eddie nodded.

"Who are these people, Jack?"

I shook him off.

"I won't tell you that now. Some of them you can guess, some you can't. Anyway, be patient. You'll get more just showing up tonight. And so will I."

He squinted at me.

"What does that mean?"

I shrugged.

"Don't worry, Eddie. When this is over you'll be the star of the Costa Rican security police."

He was watching me suspiciously, as if I were somebody dressed as Jack Lacey. He leaned back in his chair.

"It's nice I have you looking out for my interests, Jack, but I don't understand why you are doing this. It is very uncharacteristic of you. You are usually very cautious, very discreet. Friends of these people may get angry with you because of this."

I shrugged.

"These people are killing everybody around me. I figure I have to protect myself."

Eddie was rocking again slowly. He got a sly look in his eye, at least as sly as Eddie could get.

"Or is it something to do with Ms. Lara of the Nicaraguan embassy? She comes here to the club, she goes to your house and she's very beautiful."

I let him rock and didn't say anything.

"Or is it that you want to avenge your friend, Renard?"

I made a face. "They were all customers of mine, Topo and Chelly, too. That's another reason to help you get them, Eddie. These people are cutting into my business. And Renard was an especially good customer."

I got up then.

"My place at about two A.M.," I said.

Eddie got up to see me out.

He said to me: "Don't do anything foolish, Jack." And that was all he said.

I went home to shower, clean up my face and get dressed. I put on a sky-blue silk shirt and over it a white linen sport coat. Just before I left I reached under the mattress. I took the pistol out, checked to see the clip was full and put it in my pocket.

I got back to the club about six, took the pistol from my pocket and put it on the shelf in the closet. It turned out to be a good thing I did that just then.

After I did, I went out to the floor to make sure the band was set up and the lights and sound were right. I was still there when three uniformed cops came through the door, and walked right up to me.

"You are Señor Lacey," said a tall one with lieutenant's bars.

"That's right."

"You are to come with us," he said.

I looked from him to the other two guys, both about my size, and back to him.

"What's going on?"

"You are being detained," the lieutenant said.

I made a face then.

"On what charge?"

"Conspiring with agents of a foreign government."

Ray had come up next to me now. I said to the lieutenant:

"Does Eddie Pasos know about this?"

He didn't answer. He nodded to the two other cops who each took me by an arm.

I told Ray to call Eddie and then they hauled me out.

The two cops sat stonefaced on either side of me, with the lieutenant in the front seat with the driver.

We drove through downtown, but didn't turn towards police headquarters.

"What's going on?" I asked the lieutenant. He looked back at me over his shoulder, but didn't answer. The face he gave me was the face he used with traitors, enemy agents, I assume. I started getting antsy. Over the years in other parts of Central America, thousands of people had been taken for rides like this and just disappeared. If anybody ever saw them again, it was usually full of holes. In Costa Rica things like that didn't happen, at least they hadn't before.

The car turned off the main drag and entered a ritzy residential section. Then it turned up the driveway of a house and right into the garage. Another cop, a fat guy with a moustache, opened the door for us. I got out and they led me through the kitchen of the house into the living room. It looked like the set of a movie maybe, furniture, but you could tell real people didn't live there. No photos of family or other personal touches.

The lieutenant whispered to the guard. Then he and the others left. I was led up a hallway and put in a bedroom that had a desk in it, a bed, a radio. I went to the window; it was barred.

I sat awhile and tried to figure what Eddie Pasos was doing. If it was, in fact, Eddie Pasos who had worked this little piece of business. I didn't come up with an answer; all I saw ahead of me was big trouble.

Then I turned on the radio as if maybe I would find news of my own arrest there. I didn't. I waited awhile, turned it off, and then I tried the door. It wasn't locked. I opened it quietly and saw there was nobody in the hall. The guard was out in the living room. I went down as far as the first other bedroom. I figured its windows might not have bars. I tried the knob, it turned, and I opened the door quietly. Lying on a bed with his head turned away from me there was a man. As I stood in the door he turned to me. I made a sound, I said something like "What the hell?"

Before I knew it, the guard was on top of me, dragging me out of that room and pushing me back into mine, telling me to stop acting up. But before he could do that I had recognized the man on the bed. It was Topo Morales.

Chapter

—17—

I marched back and forth in my cell there, watching it get dark and then some. At 8 P.M., I turned on the radio. A civil defense officer was warning the public about the tropical storm coming. He said it would sweep over San José sometime after midnight. The winds would be strong, the rains heavy, power lines might come down and houses could suffer damage. Already the breeze was starting to pick up, I could hear it in the trees outside.

On the radio there was more news about fighting near the Nicaraguan border and also about secret meetings going on in Washington involving high-level military officials. There was more than one kind of storm front possibly heading our way.

I tried the door only once and found my fat sentry sitting two steps down the hallway with his rifle lying across his lap. I tried to ask him what was going on, but all he would say was that he had orders to keep me in that room and not to communicate with me. Then he shut his mouth. Very good.

So I went back in, prowled back and forth some more and tried to figure out this bit of theater that had come down. Topo Morales was alive even though the security forces of the country wanted people to think he had been killed. Eddie Pasos, commissioner of state security, had to know, but he had let me go on believing Topo was dead. Chelly and Renard were certainly dead, I had seen them both. But why were they killed? Chelly had been flying air, whatever he meant by that, and Renard knew something about Hill 116, some remote outpost near the Costa Rican border, possibly where there was now fighting. Victor Mena, Sandinista intelligence officer, was walking around Costa Rica. There was talk of drugs and talk of war. And I, who didn't know what it all meant, was marching back and forth in a makeshift brig as if someone was convinced I did. Very good.

I paced some more, listened to the wind pick up and the trees thrash.

It was just after 10 P.M. that I heard a vehicle pull into the garage and that's when things started happening. I heard people come into the house, voices, and then footsteps up the hallway. The door opened and there stood the tall lieutenant and his two uniformed helpers.

"Good evening, Señor Lacey," he said. "We are leaving now."

"Oh, yes? Where are we going now? To visit somebody else who isn't home?"

He didn't crack a smile.

"I have orders to take you to your house," he said.

"Is that so? Well, thank you, but I don't need to go there at the moment. I need to go to my club."

He shook his head with a pained expression.

"I understand, Señor Lacey, but I have my orders."

He stepped aside, his two helpers each took an elbow and they marched me out to the jeep. The uniformed chauffeur drove fast. The wind had picked up even more. The palms along the way were spinning like pinwheels.

We made it out of town and up the hill quickly. The route we took brought us towards the house from the back. About two hundred yards away, the lieutenant told the driver to kill the lights and we pulled over to the side of the road. A man in special police camouflage uniform stepped out of the bushes with a rifle across his chest. He saluted the lieutenant and then we walked quickly towards the house. Every ten yards or so there was another sentry, armed.

I said to the lieutenant:

"Don't tell me. After all these years, I'm being given a medal."

The lieutenant said nothing. We cut down a side path, crossed the trench marking my property and marched through the garden. The eucalyptus trees were rustling and swaying, creaking. Conchita was holding on and jabbering at the men beneath her. More men in uniform stood in the garden and then there was a guy who wasn't in uniform: he was one of the Nicaraguans from the embassy, not the Dancing Partner but his buddy. He had a gun on his hip in plain sight, standing there amidst the Costa Rican soldiers. I looked at him, at the Costa Rican cops and then at the lieutenant.

"What's going on here?" I said.

He led me into the house. Victor Mena sat on the couch as he had the night before. He stood up and shook hands.

"Maybe you can tell me what's going on here," I said.

"The lieutenant is in charge," he said.

The tall officer looked like he wasn't used to curious subordinates, but he answered me anyway after exchanging a glance with Mena.

"We have reason to believe that some men are coming here to try and assassinate this gentleman," he said, nodding to Mena. "They don't want him to attend a certain meeting he is here to attend. For the same reason, I was told to keep you in custody today. That is all I know," he said, and you could tell he didn't like not knowing what was going on.

"I have further orders from Commissioner Pasos to deal with this threat and also to bring you here to make sure we have this house properly defended," he said.

Then he took me by the arm and led me to the garden door.

"The other road runs behind the house and down the hill, is that correct?"

"That's right. It runs down there."

"And there is a path that comes up towards the house, through a cornfield and then across the trench into the garden." He pointed into the night, indicating the trail.

"Right."

"And if armed men were to come for the house from that direction that is the only way they could come."

I was watching him closely.

"Yes."

"Very good," he said. "Then we will keep our men where we have them, right on the hill here, looking down at the cornfield."

He turned to Mena. "The house itself will be a target. You and I and Señor Lacey will go to the trench now. That will be safest."

So we cut across the garden, under those eucalyptus that were shaking and moaning. We got in the drainage trench there. Behind the storm clouds there was a moon and some of its light managed to filter through. Farther down the hill I could see men in uniform hugging the ground, their rifles laid across their arms, looking right down at the edge of that cornfield that was rocking and swaying like a sea, not a cornfield. It reminded me of times I had gone through nine years before, when you spent hours making sure you didn't breathe too loud, waiting for someone to walk into your sights. I didn't like it at all.

When it happened, it happened quickly. We heard nothing beforehand because of the sound of the wind and the rustling trees and corn. Down below maybe three hundred yards on the road we saw the lights of a vehicle come around the turn and then the lights were extinguished. Maybe five minutes later, half a dozen figures all dressed in dark clothes and carrying rifles stepped out of the field into the open as if they had stepped out of an ocean. Behind me, I heard a muffled shot and suddenly a flare exploded above them. You saw them all frozen for a moment in the light, like those human figures you see on target ranges, that clear and that still before the thrashing corn.

Someone from our side yelled for them to drop their guns, but a couple of them raised the barrels of their rifles. Then the ambush squad beneath us opened up. The half dozen men went down like corn before a harvester. The deafening rattling of automatic weapons lasted no more than ten seconds, and then, as always, came the deep silence that fell over the bodies as the flare sank to the ground and was extinguished.

Farther down on the road, where the vehicle had been, a brief exchange of gunfire erupted and then died.

We climbed out of the trench and went to where the uniformed men stood over the bodies. The lieutenant shined a flashlight on them as the soldiers turned over the bodies. I recognized two of them, the guy who had started the fight at the club that night and Paraiso's sidekick who had come in the night before with Cassanova.

The lieutenant trained the light in each face. Then he looked at me.

"Drug smugglers," he said.

I frowned.

Mena was at my shoulder. He said:

"That's right, drug smugglers. You will read about them tomorrow in the newspaper."

I looked from one to the other, not knowing what they were talking about, and getting ticked off about it.

"We will explain it later," Mena said.

"We have to march now," the lieutenant said. "You must be at your club for the show."

Chapter

—18—

I<small>T</small> was one o'clock when the police car pulled up at the back door of the club. A fine rain was falling and the wind was gusting. Mena sat next to me in the backseat. The tall lieutenant craned around.

"Major Pasos said he hopes your evening goes exactly as it was planned," he said to me.

"Is that right?"

"*Sí*," he said. "He asked me to tell you that."

"I'll see what I can do," I told him in Spanish.

Mena and I got out then. I let us into the office through the back door. Mena took a seat on the couch while I had a quick drink, combed my wet hair, took another minute to pull myself together. Mena smiled and nodded at me, and then I stepped out into the club as if I'd just stepped out of the shower.

When I made my appearance, Isla was almost at the end of her act. Despite the rain the house was full.

I guess nobody wanted to miss her last show. She had come into San José like a hurricane and this tropical storm would take her away.

Right away I spotted the Dessert Man and Cassanova sitting at ringside. Behind them, but one tier up, I saw Akers. He sat by himself, blinking at the dance floor, his mane of white hair sticking out in the crowd, a bit like an old king waiting for the show to begin in his honor.

Lucia Lara sat across the room. She was wearing a black dress that fell off one shoulder. She was sitting with the Dancing Partner, who I had last seen in my bushes the night before. I caught her eye. We traded a look and then she glanced away.

Ray was working the door, but now he saw me and came over.

"You're very late, boss. I thought you weren't ever coming."

"I was catching my beauty sleep." I took him by the arm and pulled him over. "We're going to close early tonight," I said. "This storm's coming and I have to get all my employees out of here before it hits. We'll close right after the show."

Ray studied me.

"People not gonna like that."

"It's for their own good," I said. "The bar closes when the show ends. You have the boys explain it to the customers. As soon as we have the public out the door, you send everybody home. We'll clean up tomorrow. Make sure Isla and the girls are out and you get out too. The only people who are staying are me and a few customers who want a private game back in the casino."

"A private game," he repeated.

"That's right." I told him what tables were involved

and to inform those "players" the game would be in the casino after the show. He looked at me hard, shook his head and then went off to do what I asked.

Isla was moving into her finale now and it grabbed my attention. She was belting out a Celia Cruz number about a woman's love that was as strong as a hurricane. It was her last number at The Tropical and she put everything into it. She and the girls were dressed in black sequins, like the sea shimmering at night, but it was a sea that was being rocked by the storm outside and maybe the storm inside Isla as well. Chelly was dead and she was going to blow out to sea again and see where she touched shore next. She laid her head back, howled like the wind, and then she and the girls got caught in the whirlpool of their storm that whisked them offstage into the darkness.

The applause lasted a good two minutes. When it finally died down, you could hear the wind howling outside and rain now gusting against the roof. The boys started passing out checks, trying to get the people out.

A half hour later, it was done. Ray said to me:

"Maybe I should stay and help you pull the curtains."

"Don't argue," I told him. "Go home before the wind drags you away."

He shot a glance back towards the casino, then at me, and then he went out.

I went into the office and found Mena pacing in the small space. I ducked into the closet where he couldn't see me, put the pistol in my pocket and came out again.

"We're ready," I said.

He nodded and I went out.

I walked into the gambling area and found the players all assembled. Like I said to the Dessert Man, that's when the show began.

When I turned from pulling closed the curtains Mena was standing just inside the French doors.

"Good evening," he said to the others.

He gave a half bow to Ms. Lara, who sat at the blackjack table, and barely perceptible nods to Cassanova, the Dessert Man sitting at the roulette wheel and finally to Colonel Akers who sat by himself at the dice table.

"It's a pleasure to meet you at last, Colonel," he said. "We have just missed each other in various corners of the American empire over the past thirty-five years."

"My bad luck," Akers said.

Mena limped up to the blackjack table, pulled up a stool and sat down. He picked up a red chip and fingered it.

"Guatemala, Chile, Nicaragua. All those places where we have fought our small, almost private war," Mena said. "Although now your plan and that of your friends here was to make that private game much bigger and not at all private."

Akers sat blinking at him across the roulette wheel.

"I assume you have inside information, Major."

"We have pieces of information we have gathered in Costa Rica, Nicaragua, Colombia, Panama, Washington," Mena said. "All over the empire."

Mena gave his almost invisible smile, the slight pull at the corners of the mouth. The chip spun in his fingers.

"It started two months ago when a Colombian gentleman visiting Nicaragua made contact with a foreign ministry official and offered our country a deal. This businessman," he said, giving the word a twist, "said certain other very wealthy entrepreneurs in Colombia were looking for a place in Central America where they could land their private aircraft without the usual formalities, stretch the legs a bit, refuel quickly and take off again in a matter of minutes. He said these private landing strips should be in remote areas where there was little chance of being seen because these Colombian gentlemen valued their privacy. He mentioned the amount of money Nicaragua might expect for these landing rights and it was an amazing sum of money."

Mena twirled the chip.

"I don't need to tell anyone here that the offer came at a crucial moment. We are winning the war against the Contras but it is very costly. Even with help from our allies we still have to scrape for money. The offer was extremely attractive and timely."

Akers made a sound which was probably supposed to be a chuckle. It sounded more like a bird caw.

"Come, Major. Members of your government have had dealings with Colombians like these in the past. Don't make it sound like new business."

Lucia shifted in her chair, but Mena only stared.

"Officials of *your* government, Colonel, make such accusations but never present any proof."

"You're going to tell us you turned down this fortuitous offer because it violated your principles?" Akers asked.

Mena shook his head.

"Moral considerations had nothing to do with our decision, Colonel," he said. "Even if we had wanted to take such a chance we would never have done it in

partnership with the Colombians. It would have been
a very bad wager."

"Why is that, Major? They seem to be doing very
well."

"Because at the first opportunity, they would have
sold us out," Mena said. "They would have betrayed
us. Given our political differences with the United
States, we could not risk it. They are Colombians
but their partners in the U.S. are often anti-Castro
Cubans. They hate Castro and they hate us because
we are friendly with Castro and they would not allow
us to collect any profits from the drug trade. The Cubans in Miami would betray us."

He was staring at Cassanova, who said nothing.

"Also, the Colombians themselves would eventually
sell us out," Mena said. "They are getting tremendous
pressure from U.S. Drug Enforcement. All they have
to do is get proof against us and then cut a deal with the
CIA. They will sell us out in order to have the drug
agents go easy on them in a specific case. At least they
would try. Deals like that have been made before."

I stood off to one side, sipped my rum and watched
Mena play his cards.

"We smelled a rat, as the Americans express it,"
Mena said. "A very large rat. We smelled the CIA.
We saw them gathering the proof of drug smuggling
they needed to send to Washington, to win new aid
for the Contras, or even authorization for direct strikes
against Nicaragua by U.S. planes."

Akers cawed again.

"That's quite a scheme," he said. "Very imagina-
tive."

Mena nodded.

"Yes, it was, Colonel. It was a long shot for you.

And at first you lost your bet. We didn't accept the offer."

Mena spun his chip.

"But then we realized you were playing a different game," he said, looking up at Akers. "About three weeks ago a part-time agent of ours came to us with a strange proposition. It was Topo Morales. He said to us he knew we were getting involved in drug trafficking, that he could be very helpful in providing security so that the word did not get out. Of course, what he was trying to do was to cut himself in. If you know Topo, you know that is his manner of playing the game."

He looked at the Dessert Man, who shrugged. Mena said:

"Of course, the only reason one has anything to do with Topo is his contacts. He is very untrustworthy. You cannot bet on most of the information he gives you. But he knows many people and some day maybe he will hear something or be able to make contact with someone for you. That is what happened here. He heard about these drug flights to Nicaragua from the American pilot, who was indiscreet. Topo thought he had been left out of the game. He tried to blackmail us, to bluff us."

Mena shrugged and held out empty hands.

"Of course, we told him his inside information was wrong, but he said he knew it was true because he had connections in San José. He said he knew flights were being made that landed clandestinely in Nicaraguan territory not far from the Costa Rican border."

Mena made a face as if he was hearing this information for the first time.

"We heard this and were very interested. We looked

into it and yes, there were reports from local people that a plane or planes had landed inside the border during the past week. These people figured they were government planes, which of course they were not. When we tried to send troops into the area where the planes had landed, we were suddenly met by very strong resistance by Contra troops. This is very unusual. Their usual tactic is to draw our attention, snipe at us and then run away. Like Mr. Cassanova here helped to teach them. But now there was something they were trying to protect."

Cassanova was rocking his head, stretching his neck muscles, but his eyes were fixed on Mena.

"We had a strong hunch of what was going on," Mena said, "and within one day our embassy in Washington confirmed it. Rumors were being spread there that our government was involved in drug smuggling. We were sure that some kind of phony infrastructure had been built and someone was busy filming these landings and takeoffs in order to present proof against us. In the political campaign in your country much was being made of drug smuggling from Latin America. You figured, Colonel, people in Washington would back air strikes against Nicaragua if you could show we were smuggling drugs. By the time anyone started to unravel all this it would be too late. You would then use those attacks against drug targets as an excuse to bomb all our military installations. There are certainly members of the administration who would back you.

"You knew also that if you did that, we would spread the war and try to attack your installations in the other countries of the region, which would result in the deployment of U.S. ground troops and soon there would be a full-scale war against Nicaragua.

And all this was to have happened within the next few days."

Akers had stopped blinking.

"That is all very well, but what makes you believe anyone will buy this story of yours, Major?"

Mena spun the wheel in front of him, watched it spin and start to slow. Then he looked back at Akers.

"Three reasons, Colonel." He got up then, went to the French doors and opened them. That is when Topo Morales walked in. I got a good look at him now. He looked tired, as usual he was nervous, but he was alive. I turned and saw the Dessert Man with his mouth open.

Mena came back to the roulette table.

"Mr. Morales will confirm what he knew about your plan," he said.

The Dessert Man was scowling.

"But the police said he was dead."

Mena nodded.

"Yes. That is because the men you hired to plant the bomb in Morales's car were Costa Ricans and they went right away to the police. Those kinds of acts do not happen here and since they were police informers to begin with, they knew where their greatest profit lay. You wanted Morales dead because he knew too much. The explosion went off as planned and those two men collected their money from you, but the man in the car was not Morales. We grabbed Morales as he came out of the club that night. He sat in an unmarked car and watched the explosion. He was very grateful to us and given that you tried to kill him, he was more than happy to ruin you. The body in the car was of a vagrant who had died the same day and was placed there by the Costa Rican authorities when they put the bomb in the car."

The Dessert Man, Cassanova and Akers all looked at Mena and tried to figure out if he was bluffing. Lucia was watching me.

"You don't believe me," he said. He raised his eyebrows mischievously. "Would you like to wager, Colonel Akers? You didn't think your ally would turn against you. But then you should not have played the game behind his back."

Then Eddie Pasos was standing in the doorway. He was in full uniform, cap and all. Behind him in the other room stood the lieutenant and other policemen. Eddie closed the French door behind him and came over to the bank cage where I was.

"What Major Mena tells you is true," he said to Akers. "When the Sandinista government discovered that unregistered flights were being made into their territory and began to hear the rumors in Washington, they made a complaint to my government. We investigated and discovered an operation was being carried out in our national territory, without our permission or knowledge, an operation that risked dragging our country, even all Central America, into war. We did not believe the Sandinistas were bluffing when they said they would spread the war."

He looked around the room caustically at the Dessert Man, Cassanova and Akers.

"Of course, none of you gentlemen is Costa Rican and you don't seem to care what might have happened. But we Costa Ricans do care. We do not want our country destroyed. Our highest authorities were informed and were extremely concerned. Of course, in the beginning we had little proof that this was going on, mainly we had only the word of the Sandinistas and we did not trust them. So we had to gather proof. Our informers told us they were paid to kill Morales but the payment was made through intermediaries and we could not connect that crime to the larger plan. But then we went gathering evidence, especially after the pilot died."

I stepped out of my corner now. They were starting to play the cards that interested me.

"Who killed Chelly?" I asked.

"The pilot was basically killed by mistake," he said. "That is, he was killed because someone thought he had betrayed them, when he had not."

Eddie turned and looked right at Lucia Lara.

"Miss Lara was instructed by her ambassador to make contact with the pilot to try to find out from him if he was involved in some plan against the Sandinista government. He had once flown arms for the Sandinistas and it was hoped he would help. He had told our friend Jack that he was flying air and people were paying him. That's because the planes being flown into Nicaraguan territory didn't contain any drugs really. They were just a bluff."

He stayed looking at Ms. Lara, her bare-shouldered gown and her long white neck. She was studying a spot on the wall. He shook his head.

"He wouldn't tell Miss Lara anything," Eddie said. "But the men he worked for didn't believe that. They found out about Miss Lara's visit, assumed the pilot was betraying them, had him lured to that hotel and killed him. I think some of Mr. Esparza's men were the ones who actually did the killing. The same ones, I believe, who fired the warning shots at you."

Pepe Esparza was shaking his head on his fat neck, but said nothing.

"And who killed Renard?" I said.

217

Eddie smoothed his moustache.

"The first question is why Renard was killed," he said. Eddie turned and pointed at Topo Morales. "When Morales came to see you, Jack, he was desperate. He knew they wanted to kill him. In talking to you he mentioned Hill One-sixteen by mistake. He meant to say another hill. He was nervous. He knew that was where the flights were going, a place right near Hill One-sixteen, and it came out from his fear. Later Renard went to the border, where he had good sources ever since the insurrection. His sources told him about these unexplained flights. They also told him that a certain businessman, who fit the description of Mr. Cassanova, had something to do with those flights. And he was also trying to make deals with landholders on the Costa Rican side of the border to really land drug flights, refuel and take off again for the United States." Eddie shrugged. "Renard knew all of this and he had to be killed."

Mena put his two cents in then.

"You see, Jack, it is like I told you. When you deal with criminals you don't know what they are really doing."

I felt Lucia's eyes on me, but I didn't turn.

"That's true," Eddie said. "For example, it was men working for Mr. Cassanova here who attacked the Hotel Guerrero that night. They wanted to make it look as if the Sandinistas had done it. Mr. Esparza and his men didn't even know the assault was coming, I think. Miraculously no one was killed."

Eddie stepped over to the crap table where the Dessert Man and Cassanova sat. Pepe was scowling at the Cuban.

"Earlier tonight," Eddie said, "some armed men

approached a house in the Escazu section, thinking
they would assassinate Major Mena there. Some of
them I'm sure were the same men who attacked the
hotel. They were all killed."

The Dessert Man and Cassanova didn't move. Eddie
said:

"Tomorrow in the newspapers it will say they were
part of a drug-smuggling ring that was surprised by
the state security police."

He turned and looked at Akers.

"Also this evening in Washington, our ambassador
to the United States is delivering to a State Department official a full report on all these incidents. The
Sandinista government wanted to make it all public,
but we have refused. This operation was not sanc-
tioned by the U.S. government, at least we don't believe it was. We are still U.S. allies and do not want
to embarrass that government. We have told the Sandinistas that if they try to make it public, we will deny
it ever happened."

There was silence now, except for the howling of
the wind and the gusting of the rain. It seemed it was
starting to slow up.

The Dessert Man piped up.

"So what happens now?"

"Now all of you will leave the country perma-
nently," Eddie said. "That includes Colonel Akers.
The State Department is being advised. It also includes Ms. Lara, who knows too much to stay here."

I stepped forward now to the roulette table.

"How about the person who killed Claude Renard,"
I said. "The French ambassador won't like it if he
finds out you let his killer get away."

Eddie looked across the room to Cassanova.

"Yes, Señor Cassanova is the exception," he said. "He will stay in Costa Rica and be prosecuted for the murder of Claude Renard, the French journalist."

Cassanova sprang up then. He made the beginning of a move, as if he were going to reach into his coat. I was standing less than ten feet away and I was just waiting for the chance. Maybe he saw my hand come out of my coat pocket at the last moment, that's why he turned towards me. I shot him twice. He took both the bullets in the chest and fell back hard on the floor. He moaned once and was still.

The tall lieutenant and his boys came through the door then and the Dessert Man jumped off his stool. Eddie came at me and pulled the pistol from my hand. He glared at me; he wasn't happy.

The lieutenant crouched over Cassanova awhile. Then he stood up.

"*Muerto*," he said to Eddie.

Eddie had the gun in his hand, staring down at the dead man.

"The newspapers tomorrow will say Cassanova was the master of that drug ring," he said. "That Claude Renard, the journalist, found out about it and Cassanova had him killed. Cassanova died resisting arrest."

I had no complaints. It was all very close to the truth.

The "private game" broke up very quickly then. The lieutenant and his helpers carried out Cassanova.

Colonel Akers got up, bowed to everyone and finally to Victor Mena.

"We will meet again, Major."

"In another corner of the empire," Mena said.

Akers blinked at him several times and then went out. The Dessert Man waddled after him.

Victor Mena stood in private conversation with Eddie Pasos for a minute. Then he came over to me.

"Staying for a little rest and relaxation, Victor?"

He shook his head.

"Miss Lara and I will fly out tonight from a private airport," he said. "It has been good to see you."

"It's been good to see you, Victor. I hope I never see you again."

Mena's black eyes smiled.

Then it was her turn.

"Goodbye," I said. She didn't say anything. She was looking into my eyes, still searching for that other guy who she said used to be in there. She stood there a good while looking for him. I don't know if she saw him. I don't know if he's in here. She stood there awhile. Then Mena took her by the arm and they were gone.